CARS

California Stories

Also by Ken Kuhlken

Novels
Midheaven

Tom Hickey California Crime novels
The Biggest Liar in Los Angeles
The Good Know Nothing
The Venus Deal
The Loud Adios
The Angel Gang
The Do-Re-Mi
The Vagabond Virgins

Memoir
Reading Brother Lawrence

With Alan Russell
Road Kill
No Cats, No Chocolate

Other
Writing and the Spirit
Write Smart

CARS

California Stories

Ken Kuhlken

ISBN: 978-0-9965242-7-8 trade paper

978-0-9965242-6-1 ebook

BISAC: FIC029000 FICTION / Short Stories

Published by
HICKEY'S BOOKS
hickeybooks.com
8697-C La Mesa Boulevard, PMB 21
La Mesa, California 91942

"Cars" first appeared in *Esquire*; "Ophelia in Death" and "The End" in *The Virginia Quarterly Review*; "The Murder Game" in *San Diego Noir*; "The Light" in *Reading Brother Lawrence*; "Then and On Earth" in the *San Diego Reader*; "'The Enemy" in *Crime Through Time*; "Too Sweet" in *Hollywood and Crime*; "Mama's Boy" in *Tequila Tales*; and "The Curse, " in *MSS*.

TO FELLOW WRITERS

In the hope that this collection will prove valuable to any who study the writer's craft (and especially those who might sometimes wonder what to write about) I have added brief comments on the origins of the stories. You will find them after "The End".

Table of Contents

i. RANDOM STORIES

CARS

My first car was a '55 Chevy, mine when my father died. Bingo's mother called both of us orphans. It was a harsh word as she said it, loaded with scenes of derelict places and peril. But we decided being orphans would only leave us stronger.

I wedged two-by-fours in the shackles of the Chevy to give it a rake. I laminated wood for a shift knob, combed the junkyards for dual exhaust and glass-pack mufflers. I etched my name, Swift Henry, Bingo's version of Henry Swift, on the dash in glitter and Day-Glo. It was a car for idling out of the school parking lot, for whipping the turn through the gate and burning rubber on the straight quarter mile to the drive-in. It was a car for runs to the desert on weekends, friends wedged four in back, three in front to share gas, with Bingo at shotgun leaning out into the wind.

The rings on the Chevy wore thin, bearings began to thump, and I fell for a newer model, a '62 Chevy with white pearlescent paint, tuck-and-roll seats, and a Road Runner decal in the window. Bingo said in a week I could choose from more girls than I'd dreamed of. He found me a job at the

Richfield station where he worked, and said he'd help with the payments. My mother cosigned.

I rubbed it out, gave it five coats of wax and detailed the chrome. I took up with Carla, a redhead, a judge's daughter. She wore white-hot angora sweaters, and her fingers tapped nervously on my chest as I drove. After midnight her father ran out threatening and grabbed for my door handle while Carla dove out the shotgun side. I jacked the clutch and left him to choke on fumes.

Carla chose her dad over me. I replaced her with Sandi, secretary of the student council, who had turned me down while I drove my first Chevy. Now she called herself foolish, walked me to classes and gave me secrets. She told her mother we planned to marry in a year or so then asked for the key to the family's trailer at Angel's Camp, below the border. I spent my paychecks on gas and tacos, missed work too often, and got Bingo fired for filling my tank. He took it hard. Work was important, he said. Like slaves, we had to earn our freedom.

When a bill collector threatened to repossess, I traded my car's equity for a stock '50 Chevy wagon with frayed seats and oxidized paint. Sandi drifted away. Bingo and I bought squirt guns, tracked her down in the halls each morning, and drenched her teased hair. The school counselor called us mean but wouldn't suspend us even though we asked her to. So we called in sick, started the summer a week early, and shined shoes at a convention to buy tires for the wagon. At beach camps up the coast, we borrowed surfboards, climbed the cliffs and perched like eagles on the ledges, and played games with Chicano girls down from L.A. with their families, on straw mats away from the bonfires.

Then we'd spin off inland to attack the mountain roads, coast back home on our last tank to mow lawns and trim trees, to sell off old bicycles, phonographs, and baseball gloves for gas money and trunks full of groceries. Bingo brought along his brother's volumes of Nietzsche and read them while I drove. Bingo said Nietzsche was the master of our age, the prophet of strength, willpower, and obedience to our dreams. We vowed to take charge of our destinies.

Back at school I signed up for auto shop and brought in the Chevy to give it a valve job. First the head disappeared, then the cam, then the tires and the radiator. I posted threatening notes on the bulletin board, but nothing came back. I sold what was left for junk and dragged my feet, skipped classes, kicked dents in lockers as I raged through the halls. I found unlocked cars in the parking lot and slumped behind the steering wheels, waiting for a change. I told my French teacher where to place his verbs. I gladly butchered frogs in biology.

In the counselor's office, I sat mute and glowered at her. My mother persuaded her not to expel me by pleading I had been troubled since my father died.

On a Friday night, Bingo and I caught a ride to the beach and climbed the cliffs by Fort Rosecrans, a U.S. Navy post and cemetery. We sipped Ripple wine and watched the fog light turn on the point below Bingo's father's grave. He had drowned long ago on a test flight. As we finished our second bottle, Bingo forecast the day he'd buy a new car, a Lotus or Ferrari, and drive it out of all he'd ever known, banging shifts and sliding curves to outrun even the hounds of hell. We lofted the bottles and watched them smash on the craggy rocks where Bingo said Spanish galleons had once gone down. Then we foot-raced to a tavern, hot-wired a V-8 Falcon Ranchero, and timed our speed back up Point Loma to the cemetery. I drove the first run, two-wheeling turns so the tires whined like the ghosts of sailors who, Bingo said, knew everything about everything, from crossing datelines and standing night watch on Arctic seas. When his turn came, Bingo cut over a minute off my time.

Well before the tavern would close, we got sober and returned the Falcon. While we hitchhiked home, Bingo said we had better count our blessings.

My mother wouldn't sign for another car loan,

so I begged her for cash. Somehow she raised $1,000. We found a stripped Model A roadster with street slicks and a basket Corvette motor. Bingo took a job at a parts house and charged what we couldn't afford. We had it on the boulevard by Christmas vacation, racing the straightaway from the main light to the turn, a solid mile, against Mustangs, Oldsmobile Rockets, and Jaguars. I drove the setups, Bingo the hard runs, with Rhonda, my new girl, between us and squeezing us both, her thighs spread to clear the floor shift. In a month we owed money everywhere. Our bet was $50 the night a patrolman lay waiting. We had Gallo wine in the car, and my license was already suspended. I grabbed Rhonda and ran, yelling at Bingo to leave the roadster, but he waved us away. In the morning his mother called, just home from juvenile hall. She cussed at me and yelled that Bingo's troubles were all on account of my cars.

In a week he was out of the hall. We sold the roadster to pay off our debts and the parts we had charged. What was left bought us a '46 Chrysler limousine. I ripped out the middle seat, Bingo found a German radio, Rhonda covered a floor pad with velour. Bingo took the Chrysler on Fridays, Saturdays were mine, and on weeknights we doubled. Rhonda demanded the pad. She claimed the buttons on the front seat bruised her. Bingo's girls were not so dainty.

We found high times through the spring, evenings up the coast in Laguna Beach and Hollywood, Bingo in the chauffeur's cap he ordered by mail. But the summer approached ominously, as Bingo spoke of leaving town and of fates we couldn't control.

On the way to the beach from the after-prom with Rhonda asleep, her head on my lap, I dozed at the wheel and hit a parked Mercury. Rhonda broke her arm, the Chrysler was totaled, and I got knocked senseless. Bingo was safe, sprawled on the mat. He arranged to pay for the Mercury, to keep us out of court.

With school out I took a job washing dishes, mornings and evenings, six days a week. Rhonda spent her days at the beach and turned to new friends. Bingo found work driving for a rental agency, delivering cars to Palm Springs. On my days off I rode along and quizzed him on where we could go and how we should live now that the future had come. He told me to find my own way. In Palm Springs he kept to business, refused to go out the nights we stayed over, tuned a jazz station on the motel radio instead, and sat watching the streets from the window. He was a world of private motives.

He left in the evening just as August came, in a

'58 Rambler Rebel, the day after we paid off the Mercury. He folded the back seats down and tossed in the pad from our Chrysler and two suitcases he said held all he owned. He said he would drop the wagon at a rental affiliate in Las Vegas and write me in a few weeks from the East Coast.

As he pulled away, I shouted, "Loser. Deserter."

I can still see him between the lines of the news, on the grade above Barstow bound flat-out for the Nevada line, the windows open and sand in his eyes, whistling loud harmony to the radio, hunched over the wheel, watching the road ahead for a thousand miles, seeing it all but the Santa Fe that clipped his rear end, lofted him through the windshield, and planted him in the sand headfirst beside a Joshua tree, his legs spread, his spine broken backward.

I sat in my room, took my meals there, listened to the thud of my heart and the soft scrape of tires outside the closed drapes. Bingo couldn't speak and his legs were paralyzed, but he'd live. His mother called and told me to visit, to see him stiff and drooling, the empty blue of his eyes, and she blamed me because I taught him to drive then let him go alone. Leaving the phone behind, I went back to my room. My mother came and talked to me for hours in a monotone of sympathy, which grated my pride like a kick between the legs.

I packed a bedroll and a suitcase and dragged them to the closest freeway ramp. I rode in a hundred cars through states I couldn't remember when I left them, worked washing cars, changing retread tires, and pumping discount gas. I got swindled by a sheriff, hustled by a barmaid and her boyfriend, and robbed while I slept at a bus stop. I looked for Bingo alongside roads and everywhere, outside of time so long as I was moving.

Back home, years older in the weariness of my dreams, I went to his ward. I passed fat nurses with rouge on their cheeks, blind idiots grinning, senile men slapping the walls, and found Bingo faced to the corner in his wheelchair. "Stand up, partner," I whispered, "and I'll take you out of this place. There's a park down the street, girls sunning, crazy kids chasing dogs, old guys batting flies with their canes." His neck twitched, he stiffened his shoulders, so I turned him around. He was all there, his hair already thinning, his nose still bent from a fight we had lost, his high cheeks still freckled and brown. He chewed a nametag on a chain. "I've been gone, Bingo," I whispered. "That's why I didn't come. Shall I tell you about the Ozarks and Florida, or the Cuban who hired me to steal a fast boat?"

Rita didn't have a car. She was refined and old-fashioned, honest and kind in the way she laughed at the hick grammar I often chose to use and the fervor with which I argued. She seldom drank, smoked, or took pills. We drove my Volkswagen to Yuma to be married. We honeymooned up the Colorado River in a clearing with motor homes and pickups towing dune buggies. Dirt bikes skidded through our camp, severed our tent lines, and spun wheelies up the bank through the night, so in the morning the air was littered brown. We floated downriver on the inner tube from a truck tire, picnicked in the mud where willows overhung the shore. I told her I was relentless and uncompromising, traits Bingo said made a man strong. Her smile hinted that she believed I could change.

Rita despised cars. She called them a menace, a corruption of time, frivolous and counterproductive. "You have to fight this materialism, Henry," she told me, "and simplify your life." She wanted to live in an apartment above her uncle's warehouse, where we could both work and save. But I argued with her uncle about money and politics, so we moved to the suburbs. I traded the Volkswagen for a '59 Volvo with rope for a door latch and a radiator that boiled in five miles. I sopped Liquid Wrench on the bracket bolts, tapped them just so, then leaned on one with a socket-and-breaker bar. The bolt snapped, and I tore my knuckles against the radiator core. I slammed a hole through the radiator, beat the grille to chrome splinters, knocked the carburetor to deep center field. Rita nodded as though she understood. In bed she suggested the tantrum should teach me a lesson. I asked what lesson. "You know," she said.

I managed a loan and bought a newer MG. I learned to tune the fuel injection and rented a garage to park it. Rita blamed the car that I was gone so many nights, suspecting I was road racing in the hills or running slaloms in parking lots. But I was with friends, often in strip bars, and only raced going and coming. Then one night I turned off to a vacant lot to test the MG in the dirt, lost control on a right-angle turn, slid through a fence, and drowned the front end in a backyard swimming pool. "God, Henry," Rita said. "You want to cause your own apocalypse."

We collected insurance and moved back to the city. I worked overtime at a Shell station. We lived off Rita's pay and saved mine. I told Rita, "Bingo said a child moves out from his home to his neighborhood, to his town, to his country, to the world until he knows them all, then he owns them all and makes them what he is. If he stops he stays a child and owns nothing but a strict and provincial mind."

Rita only shook her head. But she agreed to travel. I arranged for a drive-away to the East Coast, a '70 Ford Torino automatic, air-conditioned with power seats and a 429. Over vacant southern highways it held the white line as true as an oath, and the cab rode so smooth we could've played dominoes on the glove box door. We dropped the Torino at a warehouse in New York and caught a cab to the airport. I trembled behind the driver, watching jets fall from the sky. Their speed and their promise were terrifying.

In Luxembourg, outside the American Express, we found a Volkswagen bus with international plates and rust holes through the doors. We highballed through Germany and France and down the coast of Spain, taking on riders to share gas and the fees for campgrounds. Some told stories about Israel and the Himalayas or boasted of how long they had traveled. Rita called them aimless.

In Morocco we parked on a beach in a row of buses, wagons and cars with tents. Beside us was a '54 Renault that had ferried from Australia to Indonesia, crossed to India and come overland to Belgium and south. I sat on the fender with Lee, the Australian, talking of our routes, schemes for making money, and vapor lock, while Rita and her friend walked miles along the beach hunting for shells and privacy. In the evenings Lee and I ran the Renault to the next camp for kif and opium.

In the salt air, rust spread like fungus on our bus. Rita said we should stay and let it rot, but I wouldn't allow it, so we took the bus inland to Marrakech. Rita turned homesick and said she was lonely. Offended, I left her alone, smoked kif in the shadows of mosques and alleys, haggled over nothings in the bazaar, sought out arguments in teashops. Rita called me tormented, but I denied it. She called us incompatible, and I agreed. She could sit still while I had to move, she wanted to lounge in bed while I passed through like a freight at a mail stop, she was kind and I was foul-tempered, she was a throwback and I was a man of my time.

I dealt us a three-way trade that gave us a Land Rover, gave the Land Rover owners two camels and the camel owner our bus. I followed the camels to the foothills of the Atlas Mountains then turned back and cracked the frame of the Land Rover leaping a gully. No welder in Marrakech, Algiers, Constantine or Tunis could bind the frame for good. It snapped for the last time in Sicily, breaking the transmission mounts and leaving us pinned to an intersection. We dropped the plates in the Strait of Messina.

In Athens I found a deal on a Fiat and a job tuning Volkswagens. During the days Rita explored the ruins and museums, and on the weekends we drove up the coast past Marathon and as far as Delphi. Rita wanted to stop at every pile of rubble. I climbed to high ground and looked east. When she caught up, I said, "Bingo told me about the wars with the Trojans who lived out that way across the Aegean Sea. Their soldiers marched or sailed for weeks at a time. They were restless, like me."

Rita held me from behind. "They were soldiers. They only did what they had to," she said. "You're a romantic, Henry, and somewhat foolish."

She loved the thieves' market near where we rented, the Acropolis view, the pushcarts, balconies, and blocked off streets. She would've stayed behind if she hadn't gotten pregnant.

We sold the Fiat in Luxembourg and caught a drive-away from New York to L.A. Rita slept across the Great Plains, cradling her belly. At home we bought a '65 Datsun, traded up for a Ford Courier, then a '70 Dodge van with a bed and a propane stove. When Nico was born and wouldn't sleep, I drove her on the circle of freeways around our city, watched her rocking beside me, told her stories as if she could understand, and sang lullabies until she fell asleep. When I parked at our house she woke again.

Rita refused to work at first, but our bills overwhelmed her, the payments on the van, on the tract house we managed to buy because she wanted a home for Nico, on toys and blenders, on a piano and a juice machine. I argued that our hand-to-mouth living wasn't my fault, but the times, the

14

banks, her spending, and inflation. I said we could sell everything and live well in Mexico, for a while anyway. She called me nearsighted, impractical, insensitive. She held Nico late into the nights and cried too often when she had leave her for work. We found a childcare center just off the freeway.

We saved for the summer and drove on a vacation to the northwest. When Nico fussed I propped her on my lap between my belly and the steering wheel. Rita called it dangerous, but I held firm and Nico got her way. In campgrounds she ran wild on her strong bowed legs, making friends while I followed behind and Rita watched from the van. I took Nico on a raft in the Klamath River while Rita watched from the shore. Rita and I didn't talk much, it seemed there was nothing new to say, but we covered a lot of ground, Washington, Oregon, Idaho.

I hadn't seen Bingo in more than two years. I rehearsed outside the sanitarium. "Bingo," I would say, "I've tried, like you coached me, to keep the world off-balance, to turn into the skids and gas gently when the wheels start to spin. But Rita calls me a boy and she's turned spiteful. She doesn't get that I've outrun history when any cold room seemed grand comfort compared to the drudgery of putting one foot before the other, when the bitterest nagging or the cruelest silence seemed better than moving on. I've outlived the days when a man would turn back to a home he despised, lie down with a woman whose sorrows have scarred his heart and soul, who has tired of everything he is and found he's got nothing left to give. So I'll buy a car that jumps off the line, a five-speed, overhead cam with tinted glass and wheels that can whip a U-turn in a driveway. I'll never stop driving, Bingo, no matter how futile ..."

Inside the rest home, the windows were shaded, the rooms in twilight and the hallway in darkness. I flinched from men who grabbed my arm hoping I had brought whiskey or come to take them away. At the end of the hall, I found an exit to a patio and a path to a locked gate on a high chain fence around a playground. Behind the fence were basketball hoops, jungle bars, and Bingo in his wheelchair.

His legs were withered thin, but his arms and shoulders were massive. He was spinning laps along the fence, skirting the basketball poles, pumping as if he were running scared. "Bingo!" I shouted. "It's me, Swift Henry." But he only picked up speed. "You can watch me leave now with no regrets except Nico. But fathers are a luxury these days. It's a world of orphans." He angled his chair and slammed the fence at my knees. He was tan as in our summers but his hair was shaved to stubble and receding. He rubbed his eyes with the heels of his hands, and kept them there. "Shall I tell you about airplanes?" I whispered. "I'll try for a job at an airport and fly for free. Up there you can't feel the speed."

His head cocked sideways then he turned away and pulled his laps slowly, like a children's pony in a playland. I wished to God Rita were there to hold me.

OPHELIA IN DEATH

There was Ophelia in a painting at a gallery in London, dead, pallid, her skirts billowing, flowers in her hands as she drifted downstream. Next were tank convoys on the Marathon highway, a Russian warship in the bay, Greeks on the corners counting beads, and skinned goats hanging from hooks in the windows of markets.

I could rave about the beauty of these oaks with their prickly leaves or the mossy pond that smells like old dogs, sing ballads, recite from the Rubaiyat and laugh in despair, or strain for the strength to lift this Norton off my crushed legs and drag myself to Susan to kiss her berry lips for the first time. But I must keep my humor. What did I expect from a crackpot and wasted world, a lair of weasels and pious toads. I'll run it all back, keep my eyes off her, and talk to this fool tape recorder. My father was a handyman, claimed we needed things to break so we'd have things to fix. It seems like half a day now I've been banging on the case, poking around in the gadgetry, spitting on the heads, scraping the crust off the batteries. The reels turn, but it won't play back. It might be recording, I don't know.

On a museum bench by Ophelia I scored a lid of Moroccan kif from Oscar the drummer. That's how we met. He brought me to Potter, lead guitar, promoter and manager, a pushy little fruit with a nose wart and the Thames van that carried us all down to Athens. British rock bands were happening, and we booked most of the clubs in the city and all the American bases. A widow took me in, shared her bunk on her sloop at a yacht club in Piraeus. She was old as Lucifer and twice as nasty with a fetish for twisted positions she had learned in a Swedish clinic, but she bought me crabs and squid in the wharf cafes, tossed me spare change for cab fares and tips, and promised to sail me around the Mediterranean when the coup lifted the ban on foreign flags leaving the harbor.

I'd show up at clubs five minutes before gigs, Potter would stomp and fume that I was late, loaded, and had missed rehearsal. I'd smooth his bangs, pat his cheek, and promise to kiss him someday. Then the sad herds would straggle in, females with skirts so short that when they danced leaning backward their soft little targets lay open for bulls-eyes, bald poets on economy tours who toasted the philosophers with retsina, Seabees who moped in the corners because they had a year left of their hitch or swaggered around as if the BMWs and Nortons they rode made them real outlaws.

In the military clubs the wives, half of them pregnant, dragged themselves in and out from the laundromat or left between sets to go bowling. The enlisted men nuzzled on the sidelines with the rare young girls, dependents of chiefs and lieutenants, who managed to slip away to the clubs and drink sodas their suitors spiked with vodka. The girls stood with shoulders back, nipples tight in their halter tops, hips rolling in time to my bass line, dreaming away their innocence. At breaks they sat at our table while the servicemen grumbled and threatened to splinter our instruments. Potter tried to chase them off, afraid we'd lose the job, but we shoved him away, touched downy thighs and bare waists and wondered if we really could seduce these child beauties and if so, would we get keelhauled and buried at sea.

Susan was one. She was Christ's sweet mother, mad Ophelia, the mermaid on the tuna can, brown from sunning at the base pool, her hair tawny with limp curls and ringlets around her shoulders. Her back was strong, her waist trim, her hips wide and firm with high dimples, legs muscled as a swimmer's and soft with virgin blond hair. Her eyes were green as an Aegean cove and blinked away the gruesome world. Her low Virginia drawl passed lips as red as the whites of a drunkard's eyes and blue in a pout as an orphan's tears. Sit up, Susan, damn it all. I have to explain.

I knew you'd ruin us both, me what was left and everything of you, and I swear I resisted. Wasn't it three weeks that we played in the club, you there most every night while your old man tinkered with his Norton in the machine shop? Didn't I leave, pass on to the next club without cornering you in the dark or giving you my slip number at the harbor? If you hadn't come downtown to the Monasteraki, if you hadn't shoplifted that Cat Stevens album, if the clerk hadn't yanked you by the hair and ripped off your coat as if you were just any crook, I'd have gone on my way, be on the open sea, playing my widow's delirious games. But I saw omens and fate at work, believed against experience and wisdom that the world was wider and truer than I'd seen.

Humor, Ramsey. But what's the use? If it weren't for the pain, I'd lie back on these miserable oak leaves and try to sleep it out. I might find a dream of those days when I met her in Nea Makri at the village school bus stop and we cut down the side-streets past the produce trucks, through olive groves and mulberries, past the hotels to the beach where the black-haired Greek schoolgirls primped on the sand. Clear of the sailors and their snooping wives, she talked about Pink Floyd, Bozz Skags, Warren Beatty, macramé, and her sister's baby's latest words. I'd leave her on the highway, hike to the base to find a sailor to sign me on. I'd jive with the Greek bartender, wait for the movie to start, squeeze across the dance floor to find Susan in front with the children and her girlfriends. I'd sit by her feet, brush her bare toes with my elbow, squirm when she tickled my ribs. After the movie she'd leave on the back of the Norton, her arms around the bastard as if he deserved such a daughter.

Did she tell him, while he beat her, that I only touched her slender and fidgeting fingers while we skipped up the market streets on the days I delivered her from the school? Did she tell him I offered, like a doting father, to buy her anything, refused to let her stash loot under her shirt, beneath the belt of her baggy jeans? I'd have loved to watch her steal, seen her rebellion and adolescent bravado, but I checked my desires. Did she tell him I took her for speedboat rides and harbor cruises, that I bought her the specialties at seafood cafes though we might have met my widow who was growing suspicious and accusing me of tossing her cash to the broad-hipped hookers who pandered the fleet? Did she tell him about what I did for Molly, the niece the bastard had snatched with no right in the world from his own daughter, Susan's own sister, and left the poor sister, nineteen-years-old, her sailor long gone, to deal five-card draw at a skid row card room in San Diego? Did she tell him I took the baby, a year old, with swollen eyes and blood in her stools for the past three days, to a Greek doctor because an incompetent medic had prescribed only rest and Kaopectate? And all I asked was a smile and a "Thank you, Ramsey."

And what will I be but damned for it? I should beg forgiveness, tug my crushed legs to kneeling, bow my head in shame, and rant about how repentant I am, how I suffer at the memory of my sins. But could there be a God so foolish as to give account to the wheedling of a con who knows for certain he'll never have another shot at temptation, What kind of God wouldn't tip his hat to the atheist in the foxhole and kick dirt in the eyes of the craven convert? Only an angel as lovely as Susan, a risen Ophelia, could make me beg now.

Take it easy, Ramsey. Blood rushes to your head. Think about the best of times, starting with the night Potter howled and cussed me once too often when I showed up late wired from a high-speed cab ride up the Marathon highway and cross town to the club. I wrenched him by the bangs, crushed his nose, and broke my middle finger.

I never was much with a flat pick, but I played out the night. In the morning I found a Greek bass man I knew and sold him my share of the group's

23

equipment. My widow splinted and bandaged my finger and sprang the news that the coup had lifted the harbor ban, that she had taken on another deck hand to share my duties, that our first port-of-call would be Iraklion on the north coast of Crete. When I told her to push on without me, she chased me up the docks jabbing me with a curling iron and called for her new deck hand to give me the thrashing such an ingrate deserved, but he was just a boy and no more loyal than I.

I was out of a job, out of a home, banished from the sloop and from the boarding house suite that Potter rented. I had sent my last checks home to the joint saving account I had kept with my sister for years. The widow was threatening to lie to a yacht club crony, an Athens detective, that I'd scored a crate of Libyan hashish and was selling to locals as well as to the fleet. I raided the boat when the widow and deckhand were gone, grabbed a few drachmas and my gear. I put my bass in pawn, hitched across town and caught the Marathon bus, too late to meet Susan that day.

I made camp in a cave on the beach cliffs north of the base, a mile from the campground at Katosouli. In the mornings I met the school bus in Nea Makri. We ducked out of the bus, off the school grounds and spent a day at the ruins of Ramnos, climbing the fallen pillars, slinging fragments of

German mortar shells off the cliffs into the canyon. Another day we bused to Corinth, crawled through the tunnels of the hilltop fortress, and shouted in the caves to hear the echoes. Susan muttered a prayer by the rubble where Saint Paul had preached, and blushed when she saw I noticed.

Rumors of war in Cyprus prompted a three-day alert at the base. Now a guard rode the school bus, Greek sentries patrolled the school grounds, and the base was off limits to visitors. I spent my days whittling sticks, scraping the marrow from the old bones of goats, and crouching behind a fruit cart in the square to intercept Susan on her way home from the bus. When they called off the alert, the sailors laid siege to the town, closed the tavernas at five a.m., slept in the parks and side roads. Susan's old man and his gang left for a run up to Delphi on their BMWs and Nortons. Her mother took a ladies club tour to Mikonos.

By noon Susan found my cave. She'd brought her sister's baby. On the beach she cradled Molly, put her to sleep in the shade of the cliffs, then raced me into the sea. I hoisted her above the little waves, raced her to the buoy, rubbed oil on her back while she wriggled in shallow water. After the swim, she lay beside me. She unsnapped her top, let the straps fall and closed her eyes against the glare off the water. She dozed while I watched, and rolled to her side, blessing me with her bare breasts. My pulse rushed heavenward with thanks and pride, as if I were the one who created her, carved her from marble.

We heard music from the campground, and Susan wanted to go. I said no. I feared meeting sailors. But she begged, and we found only Greeks, skewers of lamb, kegs of retsina, children at games, men dancing their quivering spins to the tunes of bazookis. Women brought us bowls of meat and salad and pastries, men passed cups to Susan and me. We were bargaining with a local barber for a ride back to town when we heard the rumble of motorcycles on the trail from the highway. Susan dashed for the alcove where the baby was sleeping then ran outside and ducked into the shadows of olive trees. I followed her and we watched from the grove. A Greek cook from the base approached Susan's father.

They caught us before we made the beach. They tackled me and yanked Susan so ferociously the baby dropped from her arms. Her old man kicked her as she stooped for Molly. I flew at him, caught him cross body, but the crew tugged me off, lashed back my arms, crunched my face, kicked at my nuts while he shouted orders and backhanded Susan's delicate cheeks and precious ears, while she squeezed the baby still bundled in her arms. He pushed her ahead of him back toward the bikes, pausing to score a kick to my head, another to my ribs. The olive trees stooped to bury me. I crawled and stumbled back to my cave, bruised and bleeding but finding nothing broken.

I curled up in the dark, wound my body in knots, and raged like a Cyclops. I dreamed of oar-driven ships, harpies and minotaurs and the ghosts of murdered kings. Through the course of my dreams I was the puzzled hero, flogging the enemy with a limp sword, drawn as if on a leash through time and space, bungling across the waters, calling the mutinous oarsmen to push on, outraged by injustice, and seeking a fortune of beauty.

Where I came from we drove to work on machines, built machines at our jobs. At night we watched machines racing. One weekend a machine carried us to playgrounds where we drove machines for kicks, the next weekend we fixed the machines that broke the week before. Now I'm pinned beneath one, confessing to another, this fool tape recorder, which answers only with an occasional crackle. Both, all machines, are doomed like all of us and this farcical world.

In the morning I washed in the surf, cleaned my wounds, and limped off looking for Susan. It was a Greek holiday. In town joggers in gray sweats panted past the parade of lumbering tanks and the battle-geared infantrymen who strutted behind the tanks and whistled at schoolgirls in Sunday clothes. Farmers and clerks leaned against shop walls and crowded in the doorways of tavernas and cafes. Children roamed the flat rooftops. A siren wailed, a buzz like hornets came, then the first sport cars of a road race made the turn.

The Norton was gone from Susan's front yard. I pounded on the door and waited then went around back. Susan's curtain was open, her room littered with broken records, torn blouses and jeans, a tipped-over dresser on a heap of underwear. I ran back to town, pushed through the crowd, climbed the trees and rooftops to spot her, stopped to watch dizzily as the sport cars blasted past and made the turn up the mountain to Kifisha. I peered through the fence at the pool on the base, searched the beach past the tourist hotels, the commercial docks, the fishing pier, past the Greek beach, and on up to the southern harbor. I made a dozen circles through town. At dusk I sat behind grape vines across the street from her house, watched for lights, listened for the Norton, then fell asleep in the dirt between rows. I woke in the morning to a woman standing above me with her hoe cocked. It was late, so I hopped the local bus to the school on the outskirts of Athens and waited by the gate.

She was last out of her classroom. I caught her

in the hall. Her hips trembled in baggy jeans, her cheek fell damp against my neck. "Look at me," she sobbed. "Will I ever be pretty again? There's bruises in places I can't even show you, Ramsey, big black and blue things, they're so ugly, and my face, I don't even want you to see me like this. I'm not going back there. I brought my toothbrush and a comb and a bar of soap, I even have my passport and twenty dollars I saved. I packed them yesterday after he beat me again. Ramsey, he locked me up in a smelly little room in the machine shop all day and all night, he just let me out this morning. I didn't do anything, I told him I didn't. Why won't he believe me?"

Her eye was cut, her jaw popped when she opened her mouth wide, there were scabs beneath her hair, her neck was red as if he'd strangled her. Still there is a cut on the ridge of her swollen cheekbone, and through her torn clothes a violet blotch on her ribs, another beneath the limp arm that drapes across her waist, a welt at the crease where her thigh meets the rise of her hips. I see her now as if clouds had come between us. A jaybird has landed on the front wheel of the bike and spins the thing like a joyride.

I'm forming a plan. With this branch I can pry the bike off the duffel bag. I can turn far enough to dig out our matches. I'll watch the tape reels spin, and I'll hear, because I remember so well, the forced lead-rifs of Potter's guitar, the thud of Oscar's drums, the cool scales of my bass. I'll watch Susan fade behind a curtain of flames, deny him his daughter, the certainty that I'm dead, and the return of his precious Norton.

We chose the bike because we could take it cross-country. We stopped at her house and fitted me into one of his uniforms and a navy cap. I shaved and she cut my hair, over the ears and high on my neck. We packed her clothes in a duffel bag and jogged through the fields to the base. At the gate she ran ahead, teased the guard, peeled her blouse off her shoulder to show him a bruise, while I slipped behind the booth to the parking lot, jumped on the Norton, used the key she had stolen, kicked the starter and wheeled around to the gate with my face turned aside.

We stopped at the cave, tossed some things in the duffel bag, and strapped the tape recorder to the sissy bar. On the highway I ran through the gears and leaned on the turns finding a feel for the bike. I took paths across hillsides, gauged the right speeds for soft dirt and slick weeds, relearning old skills. By dark we made Lamia, and Larisa by midnight, stars falling and the wind behind us, Susan's fingers tight on my chest, breasts quivering against my back, eyes squinting just over my

30

shoulder. Her thighs squeezed my hips. She hummed tunes to a dozen rock songs.

There are a million towns in the world, a billion villages, a trillion cottages, and one must be a place of refuge. I could wire my sister for my share of the bank account. She would lie to the F.B.I. when they came for me, knowing in her heart that I had saved all these years in case I discovered Shangri-La or Eden. I could buy Susan books, bring her flowers, dress her in handmade gowns. I could be her lover, her father, her brother, whatever she pleased. Because I was no Humbert, if one day she fell for some affable peasant or prim bureaucrat, I could let her go and survive, at least, on blessed memories.

If we could make the border by dawn, we might get through. They would look for us first in Athens.

We stopped at a taverna on the outskirts of Thessaloniki. Bleary-eyed patrons spun on their seats to watch my Susan stretch her sleepy frame. Overnight she had grown to a woman, like homeless children of war. At first light we made the turn to the Yugoslav border. In sight of the line we rehearsed our story. We were bound for Dubrovnik by way of Pristina. Susan was my stepsister, bruised from a spill.

The guards wore brown, badges of rank, armbands, and pistols in black holsters. Inside the office, a clerk stamped our passports and nodded us on. Outside a guard was rummaging through the duffel bag. As we boarded the Norton, he gave me a nod and Susan a leer. The clerk burst through the glass doors with a shout.

I wound back the throttle, popped the clutch, and fishtailed away. We sped over a rise and cut into a field, aimed for a spiral dirt trail up a black peak ahead. Susan's fists pounded my chest, she shouted above the wind. "Don't stop, Ramsey. Don't ever stop!"

I slowed for the mud of a watering hole, caught sight of two Land Rovers, one coming straight on, the other to the south as if to head us off. I swung north through olives and peat toward the woods of higher ground, thick stands where a car couldn't travel. Susan's cool fingers slipped beneath my shirt, her lips nipped my ear. "Do you love me, Ramsey?" My heart throbbed, blood pounded my temples. I jammed the throttle open and spun a circle for joy.

The Norton sputtered, missed, and bogged down on a hill. I whacked on the gas to clean it out, grabbed in the slick dirt, and lurched up the hill. They fired as we crossed the tree line. We rumbled downhill through the thin corridors between scrub pines and burly oaks. Up ahead, the forest appeared to give way to a meadow. I whooped like a boy at a rodeo, calling back to Susan, loose now and swaying, her breasts just brushing my back.

A log blocked our path, hidden by moss and mulch. I hit it at fifty.

Now she lies on her back like Ophelia in death, her green eyes open and alert, her hands cupped beside the legs of her baggy jeans, the track of a bullet through her neck looking no more deadly than her fading bruises. If I were a hero, I would bring her to life with a kiss. But I'm a pawn who can only find solace in the knowledge that neither she nor I will live another day in this depraved world.

But if they should find me here and fail to shoot, if they patch my bones and sew back my skull, if some stooge from an embassy should plead for my life, I'll find a way to Susan's old man. I'll strangle him until his head glows for the bruise on her eye and the welts on her shoulders beneath the muslin frock I bought her from a cart beneath the Acropolis hill.

Then I'll try to go where she is.

THE MURDER GAME

Greg Mairs took a Restoril, his third tranquilizer of the afternoon. He washed his face and sat down to organize bills. Sort out which they could afford to pay. Decide which creditors might allow them to coast another month.

VISA, $150 minimum. No grace on that one. Business loan for the truck-mounted Dri-Cleaner that would've doubled his commercial accounts, except he'd only had it two months before he turned into a wimp who could barely work an hour without collapsing. And even though he'd needed to sell it for half of what he owed, no grace.

Doctor Ramos. Doctor Schuetz. Sharp Cabrillo Hospital. XRay Medical. These days, more often than he prayed for miraculous healing, he prayed for a windfall that would allow him to at least pay off his medical and funeral bills. So he wouldn't die as the louse who'd left Barb this stack of horrors, so she wouldn't have to give up their home. He couldn't blame his girls if they boycotted his funeral.

Latin American Childcare. He wasn't about to betray his pledge to orphans in El Salvador. Or to stiff Ocean Beach Community Church when they allowed such a reprobate as him to teach Sunday school. Gas and electric, down now that summer had arrived, thank God, and the phone bill was lower too. Barb hadn't gabbed as long as usual with her sister in Minnesota. Her sister wanted to talk about Greg, his upcoming death, and what that meant for the future. Not Barb's favorite topics.

He slammed the lid on the roll-top desk and went to the kitchen. While he drank carrot juice, he thought maybe tomorrow he'd join his amigo James in a big glass of bourbon. "What good does carrot juice do a dead guy?" he muttered.

He sat on the porch staring down Newport Ave. at the very place where the Silva brothers would've stomped him to death for knocking up Angie, their little sister. Except James saved his life by mashing Junior Silva's head with a Little League bat.

Then James runs from a murder charge, and only returns after twenty years. He risks it all to come back home in hopes of saving his family from ruin. And Greg, what does he do? After James gave him the chance to live, meet Barb and Jesus, become a father, know real love, Greg does what for James? "Nothing. Zip," he mumbled.

He looked up, watched the fog muster out to sea and begin its advance toward the shore, and tried to imagine some grand gesture, something James would remember whenever he thought of Greg

35

Mairs. But grand gestures most always required money.

He returned to the desk, raised the lid and sat down. He forced himself to list the bills, almost a full page, add the total, and take the ledger out to the dining nook table where he would remember to go over it with Barb. This time they would talk about his death. Always before, she stopped him and insisted they expect a miracle. "Expect a miracle" was her excuse for not giving Chez the truth.

Chez only knew her daddy was sick and couldn't go on the long hikes they used to take in the Cuyamaca forests, across the desert dunes, or along the beaches of Silver Strand and into the Tijuana sloughs. She knew he couldn't work anymore, so they'd had to sell the kayaks and mom's car, and they watched the blurry TV, no more cable, and they couldn't go to a cabin in snowy mountains or to Arizona for Padres' spring baseball.

Tonight, he decided, he'd tell her the whole crappy truth. He tried to imagine her face when she learned he was as good as gone. Pale, he thought, with her cheeks caved in, tears as big as goldfish. Shivering.

His horror at the vision got interrupted when the old Toyota pickup made the turn off Guizot Street and pulled to the curb in front of their house. Chez waved. Such a beauty, he thought, with her raven hair and Kobe Bryant grace.

He waved back and hustled to meet her. He picked her up, kissed her cheek and would've held her on his hip while he carried the cleaning gear in, but she squirmed and jumped down. Barb, exhausted from cleaning three houses, came around the front of the car, blew him a kiss and trudged up the steps to the porch holding Chez's hand.

While he delivered the vacuum cleaner, broom, mops and buckets into the garage, Chez zoomed past. She was already in her play overalls that matched her dad's outfit. Over her shoulder, she shouted, "Mom's mad 'cause you didn't make the spaghetti like you were s'posed to."

She leaped over the low rock wall between their yard and her friend Maria's.

Inside, Greg found Barb stepping into the shower. He leaned against the sink. "Babe, tonight, we're going to tell Chez about you-know-what."

Over the splashing, she hollered, "Since you didn't make the spaghetti sauce, how about microwave chicken and that summer squash with cheese that you and Chez like. Okay?"

"Yeah, sure." He stayed a minute peering through the beveled glass, admiring her curves that had trimmed and defined over the past few months since she began jogging. He gazed at her breasts, which he still loved to fondle after thirteen years, more than ever since the Hepatitis caught hold. For at least a minute he admired the henna-auburn hair she wrapped like a scarf around her neck while she rinsed her backside.

Greg sighed then winced from a pain like a high-voltage whack to his liver. He groaned, and staggered toward the bedroom, panting and blowing the way he'd learned at Lamaze classes while Barb was carrying Chez. He lay down and kept panting. As the pain dulled to a bearable ache, he sat up and heaved his feet over the side of the bed. He took the pillbox from the breast pocket of his overalls, opened it and fingered through the pills. No Oxycontin, his most trusty pain killer.

He returned to the bathroom, where Barb was out of the shower and wrapping her hair in the Snoopy towel. She said, "You asked what was for dinner, didn't you?"

"Uh huh." Greg opened the medicine cabinet and reached for the big new bottle of Vicodin. A lifetime supply, he thought, provided he died on schedule. He loosed a grim ho ho.

Barb, so accustomed to his laughs she didn't question them anymore, gave him a patient smile while she slipped into her panties and lounging sweats. He swallowed his third and fourth Vicodin of the day, unless he'd forgotten others.

He followed Barb through the cramped living room to the kitchen, where she looked into the fridge and a cabinet then turned with an exasperated grimace. "Should I go to the Safeway or do you want to?"

"I'll go. Babe, we need to tell Chez. Tonight."

Barb retreated as though he'd sneezed a mouthful at her. "Greg, she's only seven. She doesn't even know what death means, not really."

"She found her bunny stiff in the strawberries."

"I mean people."

"Grandma Ruth. She knows Grandma Ruth's in heaven."

"So?"

"So how did she get to heaven if she didn't die? Did you tell Chez she flew United?"

Barb plucked the magnetized notepad off the fridge and began jotting a grocery list.

"See, if we tell her now, there's less chance it'll knock her silly. I can smile while I'm talking about it, tell her you guys ought to have a party to celebrate me going to the most bitchen place."

"Oh sure, that'll make up for her daddy leaving her." With a reproachful frown, she asked, "Have you given up praying for a miracle?"

He shook his head, a half-truth. He hadn't quit

praying, but he'd quit believing when he began to sense that God figured his work on earth was done. Though how God could reach that conclusion was a mystery. For all my good intentions, Greg thought, I've never done much except mess things up.

She gave him the list and two bills, a ten and a five. "Don't stop and talk with the street people, okay? I'm pretty hungry and Chez said she's starving."

"She'll eat about six bites and say she's stuffed."

"I know." Barb went to the sink and ran hot water to wash the dishes Greg had forgotten to take care of.

Outside the Safeway, he ran into Chad, a homeless amigo who needed five of his dollars. He returned home with one bag of groceries. Barb had already called Chez home and was helping her with Sunday School homework about daily life in Biblical days.

While passing the couch, Greg kissed the crowns of his girls' heads. He set the groceries on the sink-board, reached to a top cabinet for corn oil, and grabbed the cast iron frying pan that hung from the wall behind the stove. Rust had formed along the rim. He hadn't used the pan for months. He poured the Mazola oil, turned a burner to medium high and set the pan on the burner.

He was chopping lettuce when Barb came in.

"What's that smell?" She went past him to the counter. "You bought a rotisserie chicken?"

"Yep, faster."

"Not much faster than the microwave. What're you making?"

"Tacos."

She frowned. "Well, all right, but you can't fry the tortillas."

"I already started."

"Then stop and steam them. You can't eat greasy tortillas." She leaned closer and whispered, "They'll kill you."

"Yes dear." He winked at her.

He was turning to the stove when she asked, "Did you get the milk and Cheerios?"

"Nope. Ran out of money. I'll go back later. Say, Chad's hanging around the Safeway. How about I run back and invite him to share the feast I'm preparing?"

"Darn it, Greg," she whined. "We have to watch every penny."

He might've argued, if not for the fire. Flames spurted up from the corn oil, orange and blue, two feet high, to the cabinet. "Oh no," Barb shouted, and pushed him aside. While she jumped to the fridge and opened the door, he grabbed a potholder from its hook. He meant to grip the panhandle and carry the flaming pan to the sink, pour off the grease and let the fire burn itself out. But again, Barb pushed him out of the way.

Standing arm's length from the fire, she poured heaps of baking soda from a box into her hand and slung the heaps at the fire until it died out. The stove looked like a winter scene, Greg thought, and stalactites spiked down from the cabinets where the wood-grain plastic veneer had melted. Barb stomped out of the kitchen. Covering his eyes and leaning on the counter, Greg listened to her footsteps drum the wood floor, all the way to the bathroom. He knew she would lock herself in, sit on the edge of the tub and weep.

As he lifted his hand from his eyes, he saw Chez beside the table, shooting a laser glare at him. Then she turned and marched out, stiff legged as a Nazi on parade.

He fought a chill. Bright flashes blinded him for a minute. Then he returned to preparing dinner. He was going to the fridge for lettuce and tomatoes when he noticed, on the door amidst Chez's jungle creature drawings, a flyer from the Roxy Theater. A blurb for *An American Friend,* the movie that inspired James to dream up the idea for the murder game.

Night before last, when they were goofy, James on liquor and Greg on his prescribed sinsemilla, they brainstormed about how to bump off Maurice, the louse ex-husband whose lawyers would steal James's little sister's elegant ocean-view home. They strategized details of setup, execution, and escape. Then they skulked along the sidewalk of Newport Ave to the scene of the envisioned crime. In the alley behind Rick's Lounge, they rehearsed every last move.

As Greg opened the fridge, he recalled the rush of excitement and purpose he had felt beneath the stairs to Maurice's apartment.

He finished chopping the lettuce and tomatoes, put out the mild salsa fresca Chez liked, for which he always remembered to make special trips to the People's Co-op. He zapped tortillas in the micro-wave, wrapped them in one of the red, orange and yellow napkins they had bought in Tijuana. He set them on the table alongside the chicken meat he had peeled off, shredded and piled neatly on a serving platter. Before he called them, he poured Barb's red wine, Chez's lemonade and his carrot juice.

Barb must've prayed for patience and coached Chez, reminding her that Daddy was sick and needed their love. Four times, Barb told him what a special dinner this was. Every time he glanced at Chez, she beamed a phony smile. But their acts played out. By the end of the meal, Barb was staring dreamily out the window or sneaking furtive glances. Checking to see if he had died yet, Greg imagined.

He wondered if Chez had, on her own, guessed the miserable truth. While she dipped her last hunk of chicken in salsa, and while she gobbled her peanut butter cookie, he caught her staring at him as though at a strange and scary creature. Maybe she already saw him as a ghost.

His girls watched *Veggie Tales*. He washed and dried the dishes, put them away, cleaned the stove and polished it shiny white. Then he fetched his pillbox and picked out two tranquilizers. A Restoril and a Soma. He tried to decide which he should use then laughed and swallowed both without washing them down. Feeling a new pain like steel teeth biting his liver, he opened the box again and debated between one and two Vicodin. Might as well use them up. He muttered, "Waste not, want not," and made himself chuckle.

In the living room, he flopped on Chez' bean bag beside the sofa where his girls were snuggling. He pretended to watch the adventures of a cucumber and a tomato. Actually, he peered out the corner of his eye at his pretty family and grieved doubly, feeling sure that anymore his life meant nothing to them except trouble.

Chez complained of a headache. Barb said, "That's funny, I have one too."

Yeah. Me, Greg thought.

They gave Greg his goodnight kisses, brushed their teeth and retired to Chez's bedroom. He listened to Chez read a couple pages of *Charlotte's Web* before Barb took over for a minute then stopped in mid-sentence. When he summoned the energy to heave himself out of the beanbag, he went to Chez's room and found both his girls asleep, tucked under the covers of her skinny bed, where Barb spent half the nights these past few weeks. To escape Greg's snoring she claimed, as if he snored worse now than ever before, which he didn't believe.

The only cure for self-pity Greg knew was to shift from brooding over his problems to thinking of somebody else's. The effort delivered him to memories of James's sister.

Since Greg's ninth grade year, when Olivia was in seventh, he would've quit surfing or anything else to please her, if she'd asked. But she never even hinted. After high school, she moved to Vegas, pranced onstage in a feathered costume, and met Maurice, an older guy whose smooth talk and fists full of cash she fell for, Greg supposed.

Every summer, he saw her at the beach with her kids. The last time was two or three Saturdays ago. He sat with her a while, thinking he might not see her again. But he didn't tell her about his disease. She didn't need any problems of his.

A few times, Greg had invited Olivia to the One Way Inn to watch his favorite Christian musicians. She would pat his hand or arm and say, "Not this time." He knew what she meant was "I'll go when Jesus shows up at my door and drags me kicking and screaming."

And now, with her and the bookie separated and Maurice awaiting trial for conspiring with his Vegas connections to take over the action of an Indian casino, some Beverly Hills sharks were going to snatch her home in exchange for their fees. Banish Olivia and her kids to the roach-infested welfare apartment next door to the one where his death would send Barb and Chez.

On a sudden impulse, he stood too fast, got woozy but managed to stagger to the hall cabinet next to the door to Chez's bedroom. One of his girls made breathy whistles in her sleep. He tiptoed and pulled the door closed, taking pains to latch it quietly even though he saw double knobs.

He went to the dining nook for a chair and returned to the hallway. Twice he started to mount the chair but wobbled. The third attempt succeeded because he grasped the cabinet handles in time.

When he opened the cabinet, he bonked his forehead with the door's sharp corner, drawing a little blood but not enough to dribble into his eye. The objects of this expedition, his high school annuals, were in the back of the cabinet. He had to move things, a pewter vase and picture frames, and the shoebox sealed with duct tape in which he had stashed the .25 caliber six shot revolver he'd bought at a pawnshop and used to carry on risky assignments, back when he was a security guard.

He climbed off the chair, balancing with one hand, all of his high school annuals tucked beneath the other arm, though only his senior year would have photos of Olivia. He must've left the shoebox teetering on the edge of the cabinet. As he stepped down, it fell, grazed his shoulder, made a bong sound as it hit the chair and landed on the carpet with a sharp thud. Greg whispered a curse and waited for Barb to shout, "Hey, be quiet."

But if the crash had woke her, she ignored the disruption. He picked up the shoebox, set it on the chair and went to the dining nook table. He opened his senior yearbook, turned one page and found the first picture of Olivia, above the caption "Most Popular." She wore a pleated skirt, an inch or so above the knees, and a purple short-sleeved sweater Greg remembered he had always wanted to rub his nose in. She was made-up heavy like the Portuguese babes from tuna fishing families. Like Angie Silva, who'd simply been too kind and loving to tell him no. Maybe in eternity, over a few thousand years, he could somehow make up for the disaster his lousy hormones had caused the Silvas. Though he wasn't Catholic, he liked the idea of purgatory.

Olivia's dark lipstick looked especially exotic haloed by her wavy golden hair. But gorgeous as she was, what set her above the other beauties was her goodness. She wasn't shy or proud, but honest and gracious. Loyal to her friends, pleasant to everyone. She earned good grades without showing off. Greg remembered a girl saying, "Olivia can afford to be sweet, 'cause she's got nothing to prove."

"Phooey," Greg mumbled, and turned the page. "Everybody's got stuff to prove." He found six more pictures of Olivia. The booster club, the French club. "French, huh?" he mumbled. Something else he'd forgotten. Maybe French classes had helped prime her to choose a guy named Maurice.

"Maurice," he snarled.

Then he found Olivia in candid shots at a football playoff game and at dances. He caught nostalgia dragging his thoughts back toward his incipient death. He had chosen to use the word incipient after Doctor Ramos said it. The bookish term made dying feel less real. He craved a smoke. He kept his stash of sinsemilla and papers in a top kitchen cabinet beside Mazola oil, Raid and other items Barb considered dangerous.

He sat at the table and rolled a fat number. Before he lit up, he realized that after smoking he was likely to forget or blow off returning the annuals and his stash to where they belonged. He set the joint on the table, tossed the baggy into the cabinet, stacked the annuals and carried them through the living room. As he lifted his right foot onto the chair, he noticed the shoebox and felt a mild electric warmth. A power surge.

He managed to replace the annuals without dropping anything. When he closed the cabinet doors, they didn't bang.

He fetched a Diet Slice and carried the shoebox and other items out front. In the fog, thick and greenish, he sat on the folding beach chair with plastic slats. He smoked a few hits and discovered that tonight the weed's first effect was to revive the sucking pain in his liver. He popped the tab on the Slice to lube his dry mouth and to wash down another Vicodin.

Green lights the size of fireflies began flitting around him. With each hit, more tiny green lights appeared in the fog. By his last puff they were a legion. Harbingers of death, he imagined. To lighten his rising terror, he muttered, "I'll shoot the bastards," and reached down to pick up the shoebox, on the porch floor at his feet. But when he leaned, he toppled forward and only braced his fall by grabbing a post, just short of a nosedive off the porch into Barb's tulips.

The folding chair had collapsed behind him. He knelt, turned and unfolded the chair, set it upright and sat in it with the shoebox on his thigh. He ripped off the duct tape, tore off the lid and tipped the gun onto his lap. It was wrapped in a dishtowel, which he unwrapped before he remembered that when he packed away the gun, he'd put a round of six cartridges with it.

Without thinking why, he loaded the gun. But the instant he gripped it with his finger on the trigger he knew just why.

Suddenly as though he'd gotten bewitched, turned from a frog into a prince, he saw everything with different eyes. His chest swelled with tangy air, though he couldn't recall breathing. His brain dismissed all the dread, gloom and sorrow for a lifetime of wasted opportunities and foolish decisions. He believed the act he was created to perform had presented itself. For once, he felt like a champion.

But the next instant he thought, *Murder?*

He wasn't going to kill anybody. The idea was just another of his fantasies, like when he used to imagine playing lead guitar for Bob Dylan even though he only knew six chords and lost the rhythm a few times every song he tried to play.

The guy I ought to shoot is myself, he thought.

He tried to remember the last time he'd gotten this mired in despair. If he could remember, maybe he'd also remember a way to climb out of it.

"David," he muttered. King David made a habit of sinking in despair and climbing out. David was usually in danger. Because he was always killing people. "Saul killed his thousands but David his tens of thousands," he quoted. David killed people because God told him to.

Greg lay the gun in his lap, sat motionless though the heat surging inside made him ache to move, and counted the signs he'd been given, maybe by God.

First, James invents the murder game. Then came the movie flyer that reminded him of the murder game. Barb had posted that flyer. She never posted flyers. Next, Barb and Chez fell asleep at 8:30, when every single other night Chez would throw a fit if they tried to put her down before the Sea World fireworks.

And a few minutes later the gun appeared, after so long he'd forgotten he owned the damned thing.

"Man," he mumbled, "how many signs do you need?"

He jumped up and stuffed the loaded gun into his baggy front pocket.

God wasn't urging Greg to bomb abortion clinics

or risk hurting innocent people. Nobody could call Maurice innocent. Only a few years ago, he was Pete Pinella's "bodyguard" until the gangster went to Pelican Bay, only months before he died of lung cancer. A news article suggested Pete's confessing to the murder of a rival Maurice probably killed was a desperate play for redemption.

Greg rushed inside. He strode to the kitchen and looked at the clock. Ten minutes before ten. Another sign. The Sea World fireworks would blast off at ten, just when Maurice was supposed to leave his bartender shift at Rick's Lounge, and just enough time for Greg to get there. If he hustled.

Greg tiptoed through the living room to Chez's bedroom door and turned the handle slowly until it stopped. He pushed the door open wide but only leaned his head and shoulders into the room.

Gaping at the beauty of his girls, the soft cheeks, glossy hair, the moons of their eyelids, he wondered how such a loser as him had won the mother and helped create the girl.

He crept out of the house, staggered on the steps off the porch but steadied himself. He tried jogging, but the slap of his feet on the pavement spooked him.

Down the hill in thickening fog, he remembered Abraham. God commanded the patriarch to sacrifice his son not to get the deed done, only to test the man's faith.

Giddy with relief, he thought God wasn't going to make him kill Maurice, only to be willing.

Between gasps to catch his breath, he told himself, "Just go there, get ready." Then God would show up and stay his hand, like he did Abraham's.

The red light at Sunset Cliffs Boulevard was a dull splotch in the fog. He listened for a moment. Though he knew that in fog he might not hear an approaching car, he jogged across, hoping nobody was crazy enough to drive lights-out tonight.

He tripped over the curb and fell to his knees, heaved himself up using the streetlight pole for balance. He staggered down Newport, allowing a thought he'd suppressed up till now. The signs — the movie, his gun that appeared as though out of nowhere at the right time, the soupiest fog this year, and the others — they didn't have to be from God. Some demon could've rigged them.

His pace slowed for a few steps, and the fog seemed to whirl around him. The world had turned weirder than back when he now and then shot dope with his biker amigos, and contracted Hep-C, before Barb and Jesus. Maybe he was dying right now. He walked faster, then faster, almost a jog.

Halfway down the block, he weaved through a crowd of Friday night smokers outside The Jail, a pick up bar. He stumbled and bumped into a girl with buzzed hair, a sparkly halter and tight jeans. She caromed into a large Filipino who was lighting her cigarette. The guy burnt his finger on account of Greg.

"Dude," the Filipino said, and took a step toward Greg, but stopped when a muffled boom sounded. He returned to the girl and lit her cigarette while Greg reeled and thought the boom had to be from God. From Sea World, sure. But also from God. Satan wasn't crafty enough to arrange all these signs.

He double-timed the rest of the way, across Cable Street and past the Newport Cafe to the walkway east of Rick's. He didn't look into the walkway. Not yet. First he glanced both ways through the fog and saw nobody watching him from the porch of the hostel or the crowd a block west outside The Cave dance club or out the window of El Nopal Taqueria.

The walkway led along the west wall of Rick's to the alley and the staircase to the second floor apartment where Maurice had gone to live after Olivia kicked him out.

If anyone noticed him disappear into the dark walkway, Greg told himself, they'd think he was some drunk looking for a hole to piss in.

Two booms sounded. Greg stumbled backward, out of the streetlamp glow and into darkness where he slipped on an oil slick or something and clattered against a roll of chicken wire or something before he groped his way to the staircase and grabbed hold. He peered underneath it and saw the trashcans were still where he had set them during the murder game, leaving a roomy space between them and the stairs. He steadied himself by leaning against the wall to Rick's. He gasped a few breaths and noticed a smell like beef broiling, maybe seeping out a vent from Rick's, and another like fresh crap, so close he thought it might be what he'd stepped on.

Pulse slammed his groin and his skull. The fireworks kept booming, and Greg waited. After a minute, he checked the gun, found the safety on, released it and leaned the barrel on the seventh step, unless he'd miscounted. To make sure, leaving the gun on the step, he squatted, reached out and touched each step. He counted to seven. He tried to remember the equation he and James had settled upon during the rehearsal. If he shot from between the seventh and eighth steps when Maurice's foot touched down on the fourth, the bullet ought to slam his midsection. Or maybe he'd got that backwards. "Fuck," he said aloud for the first time since his last doctor's visit.

Five rockets boomed in rapid succession. A man rounded the corner. Greg peered between steps.

The man's hair was silver-tipped black and high on top, short on the sides. Like Maurice's. He was smoking, but he kept the cigarette cupped so the fire didn't illuminate his face. He wore a shiny jacket that looked like polished leather, a checked shirt, dark slacks. At the foot of the stairs, he fished in his pocket and lifted out something that jangled. A key ring. Greg nodded. A visitor wouldn't be using keys. He slipped his finger inside the trigger guard.

The man hacked a cough, bent forward and coughed again and again until he was honking like an asthmatic. He appeared to rock back and forward to the rhythm of Greg's raging pulse.

As the man climbed to the first step, he grabbed the rail. A flurry of booms then a dozen of Greg's heartbeats passed before he made the second step, but the next pair of steps came fast, as if something had warned him to make a dash.

Greg pulled. Time lost its authority. The world spun faster. Two shots cracked, a hundred times louder than the skyrockets. They echoed off both walls of the walkway. The pistol's second kick launched Greg backward. He fell butt first on the rim of the metal trashcan. The can toppled and spilled him into the alley.

The man on the steps groaned from deep in his gut. Then he hacked out something like "Who the hell?"

As Greg heaved and pushed to stand, the groaning fell silent.

A pain more wicked than any struck. Not in the liver. Higher. Around his heart. Greg tipped forward, grabbed the stairs and thought, Maybe I only hit him in the arm. Maybe he's only passed out. He needed to know before the pain took him under. Using the rail for balance, he managed one step toward the foot of the stairs.

The next boom came, and a cannonball slammed then sucked into Greg's middle, just below the ribs. His head tipped backward. He saw Maurice, with gritted teeth and red eyes. In one hand, a pistol shook.

Despite everything, a new kind of love washed over Greg. He wanted to reach out and touch the fellow. He tried to say, "Hey amigo." But he began spinning. When his knees buckled he was facing down the alley, toward the ocean where a mammoth wave rose, emerald green and luminescent.

As Greg sensed commotion around him, he watched the emerald wave sweep high, above the two story shops, and flood over the sea wall, across the road and into the alley, coming to sweep him away.

"Peace," Greg thought. "Peace like a river, only saltier." He croaked a laugh and managed to turn his head toward the crowd he sensed. But all he saw was one guy. Either Jesus or Chad, with a small, earnest smile that probably meant, "I get it brother. I've been there."

It's Chad, not Jesus, Greg thought as he whispered a last "Ho ho." Jesus wouldn't be nodding goodbye.

THE LIGHT

Skip and I worked at a coffee shop a dozen miles northeast of where the Pacific meets the Mexican border.

The waitresses called us boys, though we considered ourselves men, since we had lately returned from some months rambling around. Before the journey, we tried out college. One semester convinced us it wasn't the place to learn who we wanted to be. So we hitchhiked and found brief jobs in New Orleans and Chicago. As summer neared, in Fort Lauderdale, we bought an old Chevy and drove it home, coast to coast.

At the coffee shop, Skip bussed, and I washed dishes. On breaks we consorted with the waitresses. Tina, a truck stop veteran, had eyes for Skip, though she was twice his age. She was toying with his hair when sweet Heidi came in and gasped. She fetched a Bible from her cubby and read aloud, "Her lips drip honey, but in the end she is a bitter *fruit*. Her steps lead straight to the *grave*."

Tina laughed and sat in the chair between Skip and me. She arched her back so her breasts rose up. "Heidi, last night I took your advice. I said, 'God, help me out here. Don't let temptation lure me down to the Inn Spot again.'"

Heidi beamed and leaned across the table. "You stayed home? Honest, you stayed home?"

"Well, I stayed home all right, but that's not the whole story. You see, the devil came for me."

"No." Heidi covered her face with both hands and peeked out.

"Yes ma'am. He came right up and knocked on my door."

"But you didn't let him in?"

"Well, I wasn't going to, but one look at that man, and he got me in his spell. I hardly remember what happened. All I can tell you is, when I woke up in his arms this morning, I jumped out of his clutches and ran straight to here. You want to go home with me after the shift? If he's still hanging around, maybe you can chase him off."

By now, Heidi was shaking her head and wringing her hands. Her eyes had misted over. She was about as bright as the girls in blonde jokes. But she was a darling, generous and kind. So when she invited us to a Billy Graham crusade, to keep from disappointing her, I said "Why not?"

We didn't plan to attend, only to read a newspaper account and tell Heidi we'd gone and found plenty to think about. But by the evening of the crusade, something like conscience bit us. Besides, we reasoned, we had dropped out of college to go rambling and experience the real world, and here was another experience.

The crusade was at a downtown football stadium. It seated about 20,000. Since we were among the last to straggle in, we climbed to the top. From our seats, by glancing over our shoulders, we saw the harbor crowded with battleships and carriers. In front of us sat a trio of babes, probably still in high school. They looked wholesome, with cheeks made rosy from the chill and breeze, and curls that adorned their tender necks and shoulders.

Way down on the stage stood three big men. Even from afar, they looked like giants. The one in the middle gave announcements, in a deep and strong yet cordial voice. He introduced the man on the right, who stepped to the mike and silenced the crowd with a hymn.

Billy Graham followed, and began to speak with such gentle authority, it stopped my eyes from wandering to the neck of the babe with auburn curls.

Mister Graham quoted from a Bible prophet. "Learn to do well," he commanded. "Relieve the oppressed and the fatherless, plead for the widow. Come now and let us reason together. Though our sins are as scarlet, they can be as white as snow. If only we're willing and obedient, we can reap and share the good of the land."

He warned us. that the hydrogen bomb had cast its shadowy threat of annihilation over the whole earth. Sooner than we imagined, the basic power of the universe would be given into the hands of madmen. Then, how could our planet avoid destruction?

While he told us about a Chicago judge who claimed our generation's teenaged criminals made Al Capone's gang look like a Sunday school class, a flutter of auburn hair caught my eye. I looked down and noticed goose bumps on the babe's shoulders.

Mister Graham told us that, after traveling the world and witnessing racial tensions rising all around, he felt evermore certain that the only solution was at the foot of the cross. The foot of the cross, he said, was the only place where in every sense all of us are equals.

"We're all sinners," he said, "and we're sinners by choice. We choose to break God's moral laws. We become drunkards or fornicators, selfish, con-sumed with pride, prejudice and intolerance. But the sinful heart can't find happiness."

And God wants his creatures to get happy, he assured us, which is why Christ said we must be born again, so he could give us new moral natures, new affections, new objectives, and new directions.

What planted the hook in me was: according to

Billy Graham, when you make your decision for Christ, you do it for the sake of the nation. Without God, any nation will perish. And a nation is only as strong as its people. A better world requires better people. Christ can make us into those people.

Mister Graham had given me the answer. Now I knew who I wanted to be. So when he asked for all who would surrender to Christ to come to the altar, I stood and followed the auburn haired babe.

About halfway down, I heard Skip behind me. He said, "Are we sure about this?"

I didn't answer, only kept descending. Dark had fallen. Hundreds of us crowded in front of the portable stage somewhere around the goal line. I suspected the others, like me, wanted to get near Mister Graham and his companions, for comfort and to borrow some of their power.

The singing giant led a few thousand folks in a hymn. "Softly and tenderly Jesus is calling, calling oh sinner come home, come home, come home, ye who are weary come home ..."

I mumbled the surrender words I heard someone else say, and waited. Skip had stayed beside me. He mumbled too. I looked for the girl with auburn hair, and wondered if she had bolted, too proud or afraid to surrender.

Then a kid tapped me on the shoulder. I tapped Skip and we followed the kid. He looked about sixteen. His haircut might've come from a Marine base. He wore glasses and a practiced smile.

He passed out a Bible tract, a directory of churches, and a card with his name and phone number. I thought, Call you for what? This kid, I believed, had spent more time in church than outside. He hadn't gotten beat up in Chicago for no reason, or escaped from thugs who invited him to join a Miami gang of smugglers. He wasn't yet about to get drafted and sent to war. Most of all, he wasn't Billy Graham.

Besides, I glanced to the right of the kid and saw the babe with auburn curls. She stood with hands folded at her waist and creamy white legs quivering below the hem of her flowered sundress.

And I knew for certain that if I smiled and she smiled back and I asked her name and number and picked her up later at her churchgoing folks' house and promised to bring her home by midnight, I would drive to a lookout at the sea cliffs and invite her into the back seat. And if she complied, I would do exactly what I would've done yesterday, before I surrendered.

Luckily for her, we lost her in the crowd.

In the car, Skip and I didn't mention surrendering. We drove to a party, and told nobody about Billy Graham. We stayed in the kitchen, drank a couple beers and talked baseball with a couple lonely guys. A card game started, but poker's no fun if you don't care who wins. The only girls were hanging on their boyfriends. So we left.

In the Chevy, Skip said, "Tijuana?"

"Sure," I said. "Why not?"

Before our rambling days, we used to visit Tijuana regularly, mostly for the experience. On Avenida Revolución, even when nothing was happening, you knew any second most anything could. Police could falsely charge you with some offense, so you would pay them to let you go. One drug dealer could shoot another, right beside you on the sidewalk. A gang of gringo sailors might pick a brawl with a gang of locals. A drunken homecoming queen could fall into your lap and coo about how much cuter you are than her boyfriend who's gone to puke in the alley.

We chose one of the quieter nightclubs. Still, it was crowded, so we shared a table with some friendly Marines.

Skip had resigned himself to getting drafted. Neither of us were anxious to shoot anybody or die as heroes. But Skip's dad fought in Korea and wasted no respect on those who let other boys go to war while they attended college. Even before our tequila arrived, the Marines were telling us about a training film. It showed photos of camouflaged pits where guys fell onto sharpened and poisoned poles, and tunnels through which soldiers had to crawl chasing invisible warriors.

Maybe thoughts of death by poison or stabs in the dark made my stomach roil. Or maybe the cause was the sight of a dancer on the stage beside the bar. She was naked except for the panties that sagged around her knees. I thought, she could be the babe with auburn hair. The beauty in her flowered sundress could be here on stage, if she had gotten born where I imagined this stoned, lost and weepy dancer had, as the fifteenth child of folks who lived in a hut beside a brown river.

When a fellow vacated his bar stool, I excused myself from the table and moved there. I ordered another shot of tequila and stared at the mirror behind the liquor shelf, wondering if I looked any different than before I surrendered. I couldn't spot any feature that appeared more saintly or pure. I felt no more likely to turn my other cheek if somebody slugged me or to hand over my jacket to whomever asked. The only change I recognized, I felt more confounded than before, less certain I wanted to return to college and study philosophy. I thought of suggesting to Skip that we could go rambling again.

Then I remembered Jack Kerouac. The guy in Florida who sold us the Chevy claimed the past summer he'd tended bar in Long Island, at a dive

Kerouac frequented. Most every night, he said, Mister Kerouac stayed until closing then left with whatever sorry old gal had stayed upright that long. Not the kind of report you want to get about a hero of yours, the guy whose stories convinced you to go rambling.

Someone had told me, when you drink tequila, make sure you count the shots. So I kept count. I was on seven, and still waiting for the buzz, when I felt my stool tipping backward.

If I had asked, once I recovered, Skip would've told me what else happened between the time I started tipping and the morning after. But I preferred not to know.

The way I recall, I tipped backward and landed in the shotgun seat of our Chevy, where I woke up shivering. Dawn had commenced. The sky was cornflower blue. We were parked on dirt near a bridge across the Tia Juana River, about fifty yards downstream from a squatter village of tin-roofed stick and cardboard shacks. The river was low and mossy green below a film tinted with shimmering rainbows. A few women in rebosos of vivid reds and oranges waded and filled clay pots and coffee cans with water. The niños who crawled on the muddy bank had implausibly shiny hair and wide eyes of gleaming obsidian.

Beyond the shanties, across the river and the

road, a building invaded the sky. Shaped like a Hershey bar but high as mountains and made of chrome and glass. A thousand beams from the rising sun ricocheted off it.

I felt Skip staring at me. He was in the back seat. When I glanced his way, he asked, "How's your head?"

In truth my head felt big and heavy. Even my eyes ached. "Okay," I said. "But check this out, everything looks weird. I mean, *awfully* weird."

"How so?"

"Well, awfully bright, way more beautiful than I remember anything ever being. And way scarier. Something like that."

"Probably tequila," he said.

"Maybe."

But it wasn't. Tequila doesn't last.

ii. INTERMISSION

THEN AND ON EARTH

Jim Thompson in San Diego

From the *San Diego Journal,* June 6, 1942:

Novel Climaxes Privations of Solar Worker

The drab garb of an aircraft worker often hides a personality of startling contrasts, and, to look at Jim Thompson, 35, at his job as time keeper in Solar Aircraft Co.'s finish fitting department, you would not guess that he's a novelist who has just crashed "Who's Who."

The aircrafter saw drama in the problems of a war worker's family and transposed it to paper in the recently published novel, "Now and On Earth."

Share of Troubles

"The things we live for always seem far off in the future," he commented today. "We are promised pie in the sky when we die or a brotherhood of man twenty years from now. What I wanted to depict was the struggle to settle our problems now on earth."

As head of a family with three children,

Patricia, 10; Sharon, 6; and Michael, 4,
Thompson has had his share of earth's troubles,
not the least of which were circumstances
surrounding the writing of his novel.

Forced from University

The depression forced him to leave the
University of Nebraska in 1931 after two years
study of agricultural journalism. Extensive
writing for the trade press yielded small financial
returns. Stranded in Oklahoma City by the
collapse of a detective magazine, for which he
was writing a series, Thompson (who, by the
way, is a native Oklahoman) got a job with the
WPA Writer's project at $75 a month in 1936,
and gradually worked his way up to the state
director's position, which he held from 1938 to
1939.

Fellowship Awarded

A labor history of Oklahoma attracted the
attention of the Rockefeller Foundation, which
awarded him an $1800 fellowship, through the
University of Carolina Press, to perform research
on the building industry.

He arrived in San Diego in January, 1941, at
the tag end of his research. When the expected
extension of the fellowship failed to materialize,

Thompson, again stranded, applied to the U.S. employment service and landed a job as a stock clerk in a local aircraft plant, where he worked seven months....

When I was a kid in the 1950's, aliens were from outer space. Illegal immigrants from Mexico, we called "wetbacks." Whites from the Midwest were usually "Okies." They'd descended upon us either during the depression or the war. According to the stereotype, they talked slowly, had sun-weathered skin, drove old rusted pickups and lived in shacks, usually with a bunch of cousins and fifteen or twenty kids.

Nobody accused the Okies of being lazy or particularly dishonest, like they did to "wetbacks." Unsophisticated, the Okies were considered. We figured they were congenitally unable to get with the program, to wear a gray flannel suit or give a sales pitch or hunker over a desk manipulating numbers — any of the stuff a fellow had to do to decently house and feed his family, to buy them a television, a tract house and a new car every five years or so. Because anybody who didn't have that life wanted it, *we* agreed, and was trying to wrest it from those of us who had it. Meaning *they* were either thieves or communists. Most Okies weren't thieves. So they must be communists.

Jim Thompson was an Okie. More educated than the stereotype. A whole lot more sophisticated. He'd arrived during the second wave that hit the state, San Diego in particular, as the factories along Harbor Drive converted to wartime production and hired workers by the thousands. After losing his job as director of the federal Work Project Administration (WPA) Oklahoma State Writers' Project, when his friend Bob Woods needed a car delivered to California, Thompson grasped the opportunity. Maybe out in California he could become a successful novelist and earn enough to rescue his father out of the Oklahoma nursing home where, on account of Pop's health and their other burdens, they'd left him behind.

At Ryan Aeronautical, Thompson worked twelve hours days through spring and summer. He wrote about the factory and its workers in *Now and On Earth.*

... In the ten weeks I have been here I have heard the word f--k used more often than I had in my life heretofore. Everyone uses it, from the factory manager down to the maintenance men. Upstairs in the office you will hear it fifty times in an hour, and the women and girls have become so accustomed to it that they never so much as raise an eyebrow.

I don't know why the word should be more popular in aircraft than it is elsewhere, but there must be a reason. I've been dallying with the idea of writing about it — but, of course, I won't. If I do any writing, it'll be on my story. It's about finished, and I can get some money for it. I hope....

San Diego, prior to the establishment of the aircraft factories, was not inappropriately dubbed the "City of the Living Dead." There were no industries, there was no construction; the town's one asset was its climate. If you were young and wanted excitement and had a living to make, why, the town wouldn't want you and you wouldn't want it. If you were old and had a small income or pension, you couldn't have found a more attractive place to live (or die) in.

Well, when the defense boom struck, the town just couldn't throw off its lethargy. It did ultimately, but for a long time the city fathers' idea of taking care of a 100 percent increase in population was to up the price of rents and other living incidentals by a corresponding increase. Living isn't cheap here now, or even moderately reasonable, but the Government has stepped in....

Offhand, I'd say that two thirds of the men are under thirty; half of them, probably, under twenty-five. And intelligence is much higher than the average. Practically every production worker who is not already a skilled mechanic must be a trade school graduate, which means, invariably, that he is a high-school graduate also. In non-production, such as I am in, two years of college or the equivalent are required. Degrees are so numerous as to be commonplace. An average of only one out of twenty-five applicants is given a job, and fully a fourth of those are discharged during or at the end of the thirty-day probationary period.

I mention all this, not by way of giving myself an indirect pat on the back, but because of the newspaper talk to the effect that the aircraft plants have made the WPA and other relief agencies unnecessary. Nothing could be further from the truth. You find no dispossessed share-croppers or barnyard mechanics here. They get no farther than the office-boy in the Personnel Department.

Off work, Thompson drank. If sorrow repeatedly drove him to booze, as in the case of Jim Dillon, the narrator of *Now and On Earth*, two sorrows surely weighed heaviest.

There was the failure of his writing. Sapped of his creativity after several years of WPA projects, and plagued by the difficulties of his family life, at age thirty-five he felt like a has-been before he'd even gotten started with his real ambition, to become a novelist.

But the most oppressive sorrow, the one that shadowed and haunted him, was the guilt for having left his father in an Oklahoma City nursing home. He wanted to send for "Pop," reunite the family in San Diego. But at $36 a week, split between Thompson, his wife, three kids and his mother, it wasn't happening.

Thompson and his father had long been antagonists, opposed in vision and disposition. Both were dreamers, only Jimmie's dreams were artistic, Pop's entrepreneurial. In Thompson's autobiography *Bad Boy*, we find Pop as a Democratic sheriff in Republican territory; a too-honest-to-win candidate for Congress; an innocent fugitive from embezzling charges; a successful attorney/accountant; the proprietor of a sawmill, a hotel, a truck farm, a bush league baseball club, a garbage hauling concern, a turkey ranch, a general store; an oil millionaire until, after a couple years in the Texas oil fields, he'd depleted the fortune.

Since Jimmie proved as shy, quiet and brooding as Pop was hearty, funny, and genial, Pop didn't understand the kid. Not being a master at holding his peace, he consistently upbraided Jimmie for his "short-comings." Especially when, as a teenager, Jimmie turned to dissipation and crime, as a bellhop in a luxury hotel and sometime procurer of illegal commodities.

When Jimmie, entering his teens, questioned whether "a man who had made such a screw-up of his own affairs" was a suitable mentor for him, father and son squared off in test of wills that lasted a decade.

In 1925, Jimmie and Pop partnered in a wildcat oil well near Big Springs, Texas. The well came in, but not before they'd mortgaged it away. When a dreamer's dreams get smashed, he either finds a new one or wastes away. Jimmie had one — of becoming a writer. But Pop's dreams had fled, hissing and jeering on the way. By 1941, the battle was over. Jimmie had won the right to serve as head of a three-generation family and the caretaker of a broken old man.

From Steven King: "Know what I admire most about the guy? The guy was over the top. *The guy was absolutely over the top.* Big Jim [Thompson] didn't know the meaning of the word *stop*. There are three brave lets inherent in the foregoing. He let himself see everything, then he let himself write it down, then he let himself publish it.... He wrote goddam good stories, but goddam good stories are not literature. Who knows that better than I do? What makes Thompson's books *literature* is his unflinching flatly lighted examination of the alienated mind, the psyche wired up like a nitro bomb.

Now and On Earth may be as close to autobiography as a novel ever could be. The family has three kids, the wife, sister and mother, the father in an Oklahoma City nursing home. The most tragic character is Shannon, the youngest daughter, a ferocious and willful four-year-old. In Chapter 11, Jim Dillon recognizes why, the evening he announces a pay raise at the factory.

Well — four cents an hour isn't much, but it did make me feel kind of good. And I suppose the folks saw how I felt and they didn't kid me about it even when I invited it by kidding myself. Everyone said that the company must think a lot of me to make an exception like that.

After a good deal of friendly debate we decided to spend the extra two dollars on a Sunday dinner, with me planning and preparing the menu. I can cook, you know: I mean I did it, many years ago, for a living.

I started for the store, and Shannon [the four-year-old] asked me if she could go along.

And of course I said she couldn't, because I was afraid she might start something [Shannon was given to tantrums]. I should have known that there was something wrong with her or she wouldn't have asked; she'd just have gone. But I didn't think, and surprisingly enough she didn't come anyway. She just got up and went back into the bedroom and closed the door.

She wasn't around at suppertime, but we didn't think anything of it; she's in the habit of keeping her own hours. But along about eight o'clock we began to get worried and we started looking for her. I won't tell you where all we looked — I even went down to the bay. To make it short, I found her in the closet in our bedroom. I'd gone in there to get a jacket because it was getting kind of cool, and when I lifted it off the hook I knocked some dresses down and I saw Shannon. She was way back in the corner, sitting on the floor. She'd got Frankie's [Jim's sister] manicure set and some lipstick and other cosmetics and she was a sight.

"Oh my God," I said. "Now, what will your mother say? Don't you know we've been looking all over the country for you? Can't you ever behave yourself? Come on out of there!"

She got up and held out her hands, and like

a damned fool I didn't understand. "Now don't daub that stuff all over my pants! For Christ's sake come on out and wash yourself and eat something if you want it, and go to bed."

"Don't you think my hands are pretty, Daddy?" she said.

And then I began to catch on. But at that moment Roberta [Jim's wife and Shannon's mom] came up. She let out a wild shriek.

"Shannon! Look at your dress! And you've got that stuff all over my suede shoes. And —"

She grabbed her and began to slap her, and Shannon didn't fight back. And then she, Roberta, began to understand and she got down on her knees and hugged and kissed her.

"Of course you're pretty! You're the prettiest girl in this whole wide world! Wasn't that nice of her, Daddy, to make herself pretty for us? Just think! All this time she was b-back —"

We were all crying — even Jo and Mack [Shannon's older sister and brother]. We were all thinking. A little girl, a four-year old, back in that dark closet for four hours. A little girl who had never been wanted — and who, I realize now, knew that she had never been wanted — trying to make herself wanted; fighting at the last ditch with a weapon she had always scorned to use. Trying to make herself pretty. I thought of her fierceness, how with the animal's desperate impulse for survival, she had struggled against neglect and slight. The tantrums she had thrown to secure a new dress or a warm coat; her swiftness in striking before she could be struck; her dogged determination to have the food she desired — and needed. Yes, and her wakefulness, the fear of attack in her sleep.

And I thought of how, during those four years that she had been with us, she must have wept in her heart, even as she fought and screamed; the loneliness that must have been hers; the fear and dread. And I thought Why did it have to be this way, and, as with everything else, I could find no answer

Now and on Earth is a masterpiece for parts we readers experience as if they were our own.

When, between the job, grief and drinking, Thompson could summon the will and strength to write, his productivity approached the superhuman. About this capability, he wrote —

"**An alcoholic**, in the unarrested state of his disease, is incapable of sustained effort. He will perform some surprising feat of industry and intelligence, accomplishing perhaps six months work in one. That probably will be all an employer will get out of him, however, for six months plus, provided he stays around that long. For he is not building a future in a job. He is only proving to himself that he can, "if he takes a notion," outwork and out-think any top-notch employee. He is, in short, only justifying his own past drinking and establishing his right to continue it."

Jim Dillon of *Now and On Earth* can neither sustain the effort nor achieve a burst of creative energy. Life, people, keep intruding. On a wild night in Tijuana, Jim's sister Frankie goes to hotel room with his supervisor, Moon. A month or so later —

"I don't know why you got yourself in such a fix," said Mom. "I declare, Frankie! The way I tried to —"

"You'll have to get a doctor."

"I can't seem to find out about any. I've been kind of feeling my way around with some of the other girls. But —"

"I told you we'd find one. I've never been —" I stopped, and avoided Roberta's eyes. "I'm pretty sure we can find a doctor. But it'll cost to beat hell the way things are out here now. They're all getting by so good, and they won't touch it unless you make it worth their while."

"Fifty dollars?"

"That's depression rates. We might get it done for a hundred."

Frankie flexed her bare toes and looked down at her fingernails. "I guess I could get it if I had to. Some loan shark would let me have it, probably, at 100 per cent interest."

"You'll not do anything of the kind," said Mom. "My goodness! You talk as if hundred dollars grew on trees, child! We'll just make that fellow Moon pay for it, that's all. Jimmie, you just tell him he'd better get the money and get it quick or he'll wish he had."

"No, don't do that," Frankie said. "I don't want you to."

"I'd look fine telling him to come through," I said. "The first thing I'd know I'd be walking down the road talking to myself. I've got about a month to go before I'm eligible for unemployment compensation. I don't care what happens after that, but I'm sticking around until then."

Roberta looked at me. "Oh," she said, "so that's it! That's what you've been thinking about when you sat around here evenings looking off into space. If you think for a minute, James Dillon, that I'm going to skimp along on fifteen or eighteen dollars a week when you could be making —"

"It'd be around twenty. And you could have it all. I'd go someplace and kind of get straightened out, and —"

"No sire! No sir-ee! Any time you go, I'm going right along with you. You're not going any place unless the family and all of us go, too. Get that idea out of your head right now."

"But if I could get away, and start writing again —"

"I guess if you really want to write, you can do it here. You sold that last story, didn't you? Well?"

"Yes, I sold it. I sat in here and picked it out at fifty words a night. And I averaged ten cups of coffee and a package of cigarettes to every line. I didn't write. I just kept reaching out and throwing down handfuls of words, and I moved them around and struck out and erased until I secured combinations that weren't completely idiotic. And in the end I sold the thing to a fourth-rate magazine. I can't do it again, I won't do it again."

"I thought we were going to talk about me," said Frankie.

"Why Jesus Christ," I said, "I don't see how you can ask me to! What if you'd been a singer — not a great one but pretty good — and you knew how a thing ought to be sung, but your voice was cracked — you needed some repairs before you could sing again. It was in such bad condition that it was plain hell for you to listen to it, and you knew it was at least as bad to others. So you weren't singing. You couldn't, and the effort of trying left you so sick and discouraged with yourself that if you kept on you would never recover. Well then, under those circumstances, would you still take engagements? Would you —"

"I would if I could get a hundred dollars," said Mom.

And Roberta said, "Jimmie's always been like that, Mom. Why, one week when he got five hundred dollars for two little old stories, he was going around and swearing and saying that he was ruined, that he'd forgotten how to write. You'd've thought the world was coming to an end.... Now you know you did, Jimmie! You know you've always been like that."

Well — I guess I have. I guess every writer has. But there was a difference, a difference only another writer can understand.

"Oh, see here," said Frankie, "can't we stick to the —"

"And that's another thing," I said. "When and if I do start writing again, there's going to be no more of this crap. Never again, you understand? All of you get that through your heads. I'm going to write what I want to write, and the way I want to write it."

"Another book, I suppose," said Roberta.

"Lord deliver us," said Mom.

"All right," I said, "maybe I will write another book. What's so funny about that?"

"Nothing, as I remember," said Frankie. "But I thought we were —"

"I'll say it wasn't funny," said Roberta. "You might remember, Mom? He'd come home from work at night and you'd've thought he was walking in his sleep. He'd sit down, and maybe he'd speak and maybe he'd just stare at you; and if you said anything to him, he wouldn't answer, or what he would say didn't make sense. And half of the time you'd think he'd been in a wreck — his clothes all sloppy and his vest buttoned up wrong, and cigarette ashes and coffee stains from one end of him to the other. He always wore such good clothes, too. It just made me sick to look at him."

"Oh God," I said.

"Yes, oh God," said Roberta. "That's what I used to say. He'd finish his supper — and it didn't make any difference how nice it was he never noticed — and then he'd fuss and fidget around and get his typewriter out and put it right down in the middle of the table before I could get the dishes off. It didn't make any difference if I'd finished my coffee —"

"And then the dirt-daubers would start coming in," I said. "There was —"

"That's what he called my friends, Mom. Dirt-daubers. They were real nice ladies, too."

"Women, Mother," said Jo.

"Will you shut your mouth?"

"There was that four-eyed bitch," I said, "that was always telling you you ought to make me help with the housework. And that half-wit you'd met over at the grocery store. And that droopy-drawered gal — I don't think you ever told me her name; I don't think she knew what it was herself. And you'd get in the other room and talk just loud enough so that I'd know you were talking, but not so that I could hear what you were saying. And it would go on, by God, for hours."

"Yes, Mom," said Roberta. "I'd have company coming in, and I never knew it to fail there'd be collectors coming to the door all evening and I'd have to go and talk to them with everyone listening. I couldn't let Jimmie go because he'd either swear at them or promise them the world with a ring around it to make them go away. I tell you —"

"I know how it was," said Mom. "I know how Pop —"

"I got so mad I wanted to kill him sometimes. All he was getting was a teeny little old fifteen-dollar-a-week-advance, and we just barely had enough money to get by on, and he could have been making all kinds of money. MacFadden's wanted him to do a serial, and Gangbusters was calling him long distance and sending wires, and Fawcett's was begging him to go to that governors' convention and pick up ten or twelve little editorials on crime-prevention — it wouldn't have taken any time at all and he could've gotten seventy-five dollars apiece for them — "

"Well I finally gave in," I said. "I rushed the book on out."

"Rushed it, the devil," said Roberta. "You talk about being slow, now. You couldn't have been any slower and written anything at all. I thought I'd go crazy. And Sunday was the worst of all. We couldn't go any place. We'd hardly get out of bed before Jimmie's friends — they weren't my friends, I'll tell you! — would start coming in. And they'd be there all day, drinking coffee and scattering cigarette ashes all over everything, and — and you'd have thought it was their place instead of ours. They'd flop right down on my clean bedspread and sprawl around on the floors, and go to the toilet — and you could hear them going, Mom. They'd go in there and leave the door wide open and holler in to the front room when they had anything to say. And if they wanted something to eat, they just went right into the kitchen and helped themselves."

"Well, I got rid of them."

"Yes, you got rid of them! After —"

"I got rid of them ... and the book."

"And after you'd put me through all that, the book wasn't published!"

"Wasn't it?" I said. "I'd forgotten. It must have been quite a disappointment to you."

"Well," said Roberta, "I couldn't help it."

"Funny how it slipped my mind," I said. "But of course I wasn't really interested in the thing."

Roberta's mouth shut, and there was the old helpless puzzled look around it. "I don't know why I can't ever say anything —"

"You're doing fine, honey. You've said quite a bit."

"Jimmie," said Frankie, "give up. What I want to know is —"

"I think that's the thing to do, Jimmie," said Mom, plucking absently at a safety pin in her dress.

"What — give up? I already have."

I knew that wasn't what she meant. She'd been having a long discussion with me — even if I hadn't heard it — and she (we) had reached a satisfactory conclusion. I knew it, but I wouldn't admit it. That is one trick of Mom's that exasperates me.

"Do what?" I said. "What are you talking about anyway?"

"Why — about the story. We can send it to this last magazine, they liked your work so well, and we could have a check back inside of a month. Frankie would pay you back, of course, but it would save borrowing from ..."

I looked at her. I looked at Frankie and Roberta. Jo was grinning. Everyone else, apparently, seemed to think it was all right. Mom had pulled a rabbit out of a hat. She had dived down into the muck and come up with a diamond.

"Well, I will be goddamned!" I said. "I will be damned by all the saints and Christ and Mary. They can damn me individually and collectively and I will not say a word. They can come in pairs and squads and regiments, in trucks and sidecars, on roller skates and bicycles, and they can damn me to their heart's content! What in the name of —"

I got the bottle out of the kitchen and had a slug.

"Don't pay any attention to him, Mom," said Roberta. "He's just acting crazy."

"Now look," I said. "Once and for all, I am not —"

"Jimmie! You're spilling that stuff all over the rug!"

"— I positively will not write another story. I'll peck horse-turds with the sparrows —"

"Jimmie! You dirty thing!"

"I'll swill slop with the hogs; I'll peddle French postcards; I'll bend over bathtubs —"

"Jimmie!"

"I'll adopt Frankie's triplets or whatever she has and give them the same thoughtful and tender rearing I'd give my own. But I will not — I utterly by God will not write another story!"

I sat down again.

"He means he won't write another story," Frankie remarked idly to Roberta.

"Oh," said Roberta.

"Well," said Mom. "I don't see why not."

I choked on the drink I was taking.

"Mom," said Frankie.

"Well, I don't," said Mom. "Of course, this isn't the best place in the world to write, but you

91

can't always have things just like you want them. Why look at the way Jack London did, Jimmie! He —"

"Now just a minute," I said. "I want to introduce a piece of evidence."

[He goes to another room and returns.]

"Will you look at this for just a minute?"

Mom looked at the black-and-white Photostat and handed it back. "I don't see what your birth certificate has to do with it."

"It establishes the fact that I am not Jack London? It proves conclusively that I am not Jack London, but a guy named James Dillon? It —"

"You'd better stop acting so crazy, Jimmie," said Roberta. "You know how you'll get."

"No, you're not Jack London," said Mom, fumbling faster with the safety pin. "Jack London didn't give up just because he didn't have everything right like he wanted it. He wrote on fishing boats and in lumber camps and —"

"And I wrote in caddie houses and hotel locker rooms and out on the pipeline; I wrote between orders of scrambled eggs and hot beef sandwiches; I wrote in the checkroom of a dance hall; I wrote in my car while I was chasing down deadbeats and skips; I wrote while I was chopping dough in a bakery. I held five different jobs at one time and I went to school, and I wrote. I wrote a story every day for thirty days. I wrote —"

"I think we'd all better go to bed," said Roberta. "Come on, hon —"

"I will not go to bed!"

"I didn't mean anything," said Mom. "I was just saying —"

"You didn't read your Jack London far enough. He began slipping off the deep end when he was thirty. Well I'm thirty-five. Thirty-five, can you understand that? And I've written three times as much as London wrote. I —"

"Let's skip it," said Frankie.

"You skip it! Skip through fifteen million words for the Writers' Project. Skip through a half million for the foundation. Skip through the back numbers of five strings of magazines. Skip through forty, fifty, yes, seventy-five thousand words a week, week after week, for the trade journals. Skip through thirty-six hours of radio continuity. Do you know what that means — thirty-six hours? Did you ever sit down and write thirty-six hours of conversation? Conversation that had to sparkle; had to make people laugh or cry; had to keep them from turning to another station. Did you? Did you?"

"Please, Jimmie ...

"Of course you didn't. Why should you? What would it get you? What did it get me? Shall I tell you? You're damned right I shall. It got me a ragged ass and beans three times a week. It got me haircuts in barber colleges. It got me piles that you could stack washers on. It got me a lung that isn't even bad enough to kill me. It got me in a dump with six strangers. It got me in jail forty-eight hours a week and a lunatic asylum on Sunday. It got me whisky, yes, and cigarettes, yes, and a woman to sleep with, yes. It got me twenty-five thousand reminders ten million times a day that nothing I'd done meant anything. It got me this, this extraordinarily valuable, this priceless piece of information that I'm not ...

I opened my eyes and said, "Jack London."

I was sitting on the divan. Roberta had her arm around me. Frankie was holding out a drink.

"I'm sorry," I said. "I guess I slopped over."

"I didn't mean you hadn't worked hard," said Mom. "I know how hard you've worked."

"You'd better go to bed, Mom," said Frankie. "I'm going to turn in as soon as —"

"No, I'm all right," I said. "Now that we've buried the dead, let's take up the living. What do you think we'd better do, Frankie?"

In early September of 1941, Jim Thompson decided he could wait no longer before rescuing his father from the rest home. He caught a bus for New York in search of a writing job through which he could save enough to spring his father and care for him. On the way to New York, he laid over in Oklahoma City to visit Pop. In his novel *Roughneck*, he fictionalized the encounter —

He could not believe it was I when I first walked in on him. The seven long, lonely months must have seemed like years to him, and I think he had begun to feel we had abandoned him.

I made him understand the truth: that his remaining here was due to circumstances beyond our control.

"Well, it's all over now," he said. "You just help me get my things together, and I'll clear out of here right now."

"Pop," I said. "I —"

"Well?" He looked at me. "You're going to take me away, aren't you? That's why you've come back?"

I hesitated. Then, I said, yes, that was why. "But I can't go with you, Pop. I'm on my way to New York."

"Oh?" He frowned troubledly. "Well, I guess I

could travel by myself if —"

"I've got a swell job there," I lied. "Give me —
Well, just give me a month and I can send you to
California by stateroom. Get you a nurse if you
need one. But the best I can do now is a bus
ticket."

"I don't know," he said dubiously. "I'm afraid
the doctor ... I'm afraid I couldn't ..." He sat
back down on the bed. "You're sure, Jimmie. If I
wait another month, you'll —"

"That's a promise. And I never break a
promise."

In New York, Thompson gathered together enough
of the story of *Now and On Earth* to convince
Modern Age, a small publishing house, to stake him
to a hotel room, food, paper and a typewriter for a
few weeks. Between September and December when
he returned to San Diego shortly after the bombing
of Pearl Harbor, Thompson completed the novel.
Michael J. McCauley, Thompson's biographer,
speculates that writing the first draft of *Now and On
Earth* probably took him three weeks. Apparently he
delivered the manuscript to his publisher, Modern
Age, and collapsed. Over the next two weeks, while
he recovered from nervous exhaustion in Bellevue
Hospital, Modern Age enlisted writers Richard
Wright and Louis Bromfield to evaluate the

manuscript. From *Roughneck* —

I started across town toward my rooming house, worrying again — continuing to worry. It was a day short of five weeks, since I had left Oklahoma. Not much over a month, to be sure, but to an old man who secretly feared that he might be forsaken ... I reached Fifth Avenue. Instead of crossing it, I suddenly turned and headed uptown. Surely the publisher would be able to make his decision by this time. By God, he simply *had* to.

Well, he had.

He walked me into his office, his arm around my shoulders. "Got some good reports from Louis and Dick. They're going to fix us up with blurbs to put on the cover ... Now, I do feel that quite a few revisions are necessary. There are a couple of chapters I'd like to see excised, and new ones substituted. But —"

"Oh," I said, pretty drearily. "Then it'll still be quite a while before —"

"What? Oh, no, we'll pay you for it right now. We're definitely accepting it. Incidentally, when you get this one out of the way, we'll be glad to — Yes?"

The receptionist was standing in the doorway. She murmured an apology, held out a Western

Union envelope. "This came yesterday, Mr. Thompson. I tried to reach you by phone, but —"

"It must be from my mother," I said. "I wasn't sure how long I'd be at that rooming house, so I told her to — to —"

I ripped the envelope open.

I stared down at the message.

Blindly. Stricken motionless.

"Bad news?" The publisher's hushed voice.

"My father," I said. "He died two days ago."

Thompson's sister Freddie recalled him saying their father died of a broken heart. The death certificate lists the cause of death as pneumonia.

Thompson returned to his rooming house and began the revisions of *Now and On Earth,* the elation of finally realizing his dream of becoming a published novelist crushed beneath the failure to rescue his father. In the things that mattered most, in critical times, in the stuff closest to his heart ...

What gives *Now and On Earth* its poignancy is the relentless, brutal portrayal of a man who has realized the futility of striving.

With Modern Age awaiting his next novel, Thompson set to work on the story that would appear years later as *Nothing More Than Murder*. The small advances he got from sending chapters to Modern Age as he finished them, along with a salary from Solar Aircraft where he'd found employment as a timekeeper, paid the family expenses and gave him drinking money, until Modern Age folded. A year or so after Pearl Harbor, the military had drafted most of the principals of the publishing house.

So in 1944, at age 37, Thompson became a Marine. He lasted twelve weeks, plus a few in the infirmary, with rheumatic fever. After the discharge, he spent most of that summer recuperating at home, while his family got by on the salary Alberta made as a switchboard operator at Solar Aircraft.

Jim's mother's health was failing. When she died in early 1945, Jim not only suffered from the loss but from concern for his children, particularly Sharon, the eight-year-old, who had lit a candle at the Catholic church, believing the act would save her grandmother. According to Sharon [whom I can't help but think of as Shannon, the desperate four-year-old in *Now and On Earth*], "Daddy was terribly worried that grandma's death, after I lit candles, would undermine my faith. Daddy didn't go to church, but we had long discussions about religion. He believed in God, though he used to tease my mom about her Catholicism by saying he couldn't get into heaven because he wasn't baptized, though he had been. When he was in the hospital, ministers and priests and rabbis would come around asking if he'd like them to pray for him. He'd say, 'It couldn't hurt.'"

Since his literary agent had failed to sell *Nothing More Than Murder*, in January, 1945, Thompson rode the train to New York. He went knocking on publisher's doors. Finding no interest in his murder story, he pitched the idea for an historical novel to a small publisher named Greenberg, who staked him to hotel room, food, cigarettes and whiskey. Over eight weeks, Thompson wrote *Heed the Thunder*, a family saga in which the main character presents a view that would inform most of his later work.

The family's patriarch, Lincoln Fargo, declares:

We don't ever learn. There ain't none of us can tell whether it'll rain the next day or not. We don't know whether our kids are goin' to be boys or girls. Or why the world turns one way instead of another. Or the what or why or when of anything. Hindsight's the only gift we got, except on one thing. On that, we're all prophets.

We know what's in the other fellow's mind. It don't make difference that we've never seen him before, or whatever. We know that he's out to do us if he gets the chance.

Back in San Diego, Thompson made his living

writing true crime stories and taking odd jobs. When his new book appeared, the *San Diego Tribune* reviewed it:

Heed the Thunder, the second published novel by Jim Thompson is a serious study of the transition from hand to machine industry, illustrated by the life of a small Nebraska town from 1907 to 1914, showing the sacrifice of land and human resources to the "immediate dollar."

A tall, slender, greying man, Thompson, 40, started writing when he was a 15-year-old schoolboy in Andarko, Oklahoma, and has since written an estimated 7,000,000 words in novel, poetry, articles and other literary production.

He makes long studies of his subjects in his San Diego home, then goes to New York, locks himself in a hotel room, works 16 to 18 hours a day and turns out a 100,000 word novel in five weeks.

What is his advice to youngsters seeking writing careers? "Take up plumbing." He grins.

Next he revised *Nothing More Than Murder* and gathered more rejections. In 1947, he took a job as a rewrite man with the *San Diego Journal*.

Lionel Van Deerlin, who worked with him at the *Journal*, remembers him as, "A proper fellow, meticulous dresser. Never sloppy. He often wore tweeds. His voice was a degree or two below normal. He spoke in parsed sentences and wasn't a trigger ready humorist, but he had a droll wit and could see irony everywhere. He was a very, very pleasant person to be around.

"He was a gifted rewrite man and feature writer. There was a story about a boy dying, four or five paragraphs, I remember one morning just after he finished, sitting there reading it. I found myself weeping.

"One of a kind, a very fine man, though he had a problem staying sober. On several occasions, I'd get a call early morning and go pick him up at a building — I think it's a bed and breakfast now. Then it was a drying out establishment. I'd pick him up there and take him to work.

"Once a new owner, Captain Kennedy, came in to the city room and bawled Jim out for something. We knew what would come of that, and we were right. By afternoon, Jim was drunk."

About her father's drinking, Sharon Reed concludes, "Daddy was what I guess they call an episodic alcoholic, but when he was writing he kept a good schedule, just like somebody that held a regular job. He would write at regular times, and take breaks and eat lunch. Drinking would never interfere with his writing. And he never acted mean when he drank. Although, sometimes drinking would give him telephonitis. He'd call people and talk forever. For a year while we lived in San Diego he didn't drink. The program he was in gave him a one-year-sober birthday party."

When Thompson lost his job at *Journal*, it was one more dark night of the soul. Then came the miracle.

Nothing More Than Murder got accepted by Harper's, a publisher so prestigious Thompson hadn't bothered to submit to them until Alberta, his wife, insisted, after all the lesser houses had turned him down.

Nothing More Than Murder begins the string of novels upon which Thompson's fame and reputation hang. They are called "Noir". They are akin to nightmares, and commonly told by psychopaths.

Joe Wilmot, who narrates *Nothing More Than Murder*, is a witty, shrewd and likeable man, the kind with whom you'd enjoy swapping lies over drinks. He runs a movie theater in a small town. His wife originally owned the theater. Now they're partners. She engages a housekeeper, a dull, homely but voluptuous young woman, whom Joe seduces. The wife learns about the affair and makes up her mind to leave Joe. But she wants the money from the business and he won't give it up. So a murder is required.

Thompson's challenge as a storyteller is to make the psychopath real. He meets the challenge by showing that Joe's tragic flaw isn't some inhuman quirk but one we all possess to some degree — the ability to disregard the value of other human beings, to think of them as objects who either should serve our needs or disappear.

Lou Ford, the maniac sheriff of *The Killer Inside Me*, is a bright and learned man who masquerades as a bumpkin in order to cover for himself, after the "sickness" first appears during his adolescence. At age thirteen, he seduces (or gets seduced by) his father's mistress. A couple years later, he molests a little girl. To protect Lou, his brother takes the blame. Later a town big shot sees to the murder of Lou's brother for business reasons. So Lou goes after the big shot by murdering his son who is in love with the same prostitute who has reawakened Lou's "sickness." He has to kill them both. He doesn't want to, but he has to. He also has to kill his long time girlfriend, and a hobo who catches on to his deeds, and a young man who idolizes him but stumbles into the way. Occasionally, Lou exhibits homicidal rage. Other times he simply accomplishes what has to be done. When sorrow appears, it's over the fact that our world is a grim place where people won't let you be.

In *The Grifters,* Thompson carries to its extreme narcissism and the suspicion that all we know is that people are out to do us. Lilly Dillon, a glamorous con and mother of con man Roy Dillon, grows to believe so certainly that Roy is out to steal her blind, she destroys him. Of all the hard cases in all the tough books, Lilly Dillon gets the prize.

Reading Jim Thompson's books, you might wonder what kind of sinister mind conceived them. But Sharon Reed remembers her father as "... always gentle and kind, not at all like many of his books. He was very quiet and usually happy. He was patriotic. He was a great cook. As a dad, they don't come any better. He had integrity that you wouldn't believe. If he shook hands on something, that was it, which got him into lots of trouble, financially, in Hollywood.

"People seem to think all the stories my father wrote were true, as if they've forgotten he was a novelist, a *fiction* writer."

Somebody wrote, for the *New York Review of Books*, "Thompson loudly proclaims that he is damned and proud of it."

I hope the *Review* fired that nitwit.

Thompson wrote as though fighting his way out of hell, by tenaciously seeking the truth. A more ruthlessly honest storyteller may never have lived. He revealed things about humanity that many of us

can't bear to know. You need guts just to read Jim
Thompson. Because he declares and convinces that
at some essential level you're no better than Lou
Ford, Joe Wilmot or Lilly Dillon — a twist of fate, a
few betrayals, and you could be them.

Thompson might scare the devil out of you.

iii. THE HICKEYS

Sylvia Curtis, inspiration for the jazz singer most prominently featured in *The Venus Deal*, told me hours of stories about San Diego during WWII. Also, on dubious youthful adventures and for playing baseball, I spent lots of days and nights in Tijuana. I found the place both hellish and fascinating and, in the context of Sylvia's stories, began to wonder what the border and Tijuana were like during WWII.

My friend Don Merritt had recently made decent money writing adventure novels. I needed money, having given up a tenured professorship so I could live near my kids, Darcy and Cody, whom I treasure more than work or money.

When Don convinced me to write an adventure novel, I thought, hmm, Tijuana, WWII. And when I needed a protagonist, Tom Hickey showed up and proved to be rather like a cross between my father and my father-in-law, both of whom had told of adventures during WWII.

I wrote the story and sent it to my agent, who informed me it wasn't a genre adventure story, but a literary novel. Then a friend I trusted more than I trusted the agent told me it was actually a mystery. He directed me to a contest, which I won.

By then, I was so fond of Tom, I decided to give him a family, a history, and a future. He lives in seven novels, so far.

THE ENEMY

Tom Hickey batted smoke away and caught a breath. His little office, once a pantry, had no vent. He tamped out his pipe and stared at the door, thinking he ought to open it and trade pipe smoke for kitchen fumes. Nope, he decided, better to choke in here than to listen to a nightclub crowd knocking Japs. And if he ducked outside for a walk, any way he turned there would be families dragging themselves or getting herded toward the roundup, grinding their teeth, slapping away tears. Kids younger than his daughter would cover their eyes until he passed, so they wouldn't have to look at the enemy.

The mood he was in, there seemed no refuge from the wretched state into which the world had careened. If he took the night off and went home to his wife in their cottage on the bay, he would likely find Madeline surrounded by neighbor ladies arguing about the relocation. She would hold to the party line. War's war. Any suspicious characters, you disarm. Madeline was the realist in the family.

Suppose he took a walk on the beach, then he would envision the battles across the sea, on Bataan, Corregidor and other islands that used to sound like paradise. And he would feel like a weasel for sitting it out. Sure, they tagged him unfit, but he could serve in the merchant marine or even labor at a defense plant. Being thirty-six and a borderline diabetic didn't give a man license to stuff his pockets with blood money. To sit counting the loot, sipping Dewar's, and smoking out the office of Rudy's Hacienda, while at the same time flames leap from isle to isle across the Coral Sea. While, only blocks away, the Japanese Americans are boarding the busses that will dump them into a holding area at the Santa Anita racetrack until they get shuttled off to God knows where.

Tonight he had counted a four-inch high stack of bills. Twelve hundred dollars in one afternoon and early dinner. The best Saturday since December when Rudy's opened for business, and all on account of the roundup. The spectacle had drawn rubbernecks and vultures from south to the border, east to the mountains, north half way to Los Angeles. Watching other people's misery appeared to whet the appetite for food and drink.

A fist attacked the door, pounding so long and hard the noise drowned Tom's first command to enter. At the second round of knocks, he shouted, "What?"

The door flew open and into the coat rack, knocking a hat to the floor. Larry the bouncer strode to the desk, leaned his arms and whole weight on it. He had the face of a heavyweight brawler, only now it looked crimped and timid. His voice, which usually bellowed, was hardly more than a peep. "Boss, some guy knocked off Mel, down at the corner, and bagged the dough."

Tom sprang up. "You sure Mel's dead?"

"Not positive, I guess. But he stopped squirming. Lola called the cops. I heard an ambulance siren."

On the supper club floor, things were as usual around seven p.m. on a Saturday. Every table occupied. Naval officers and their wives or dates. Older men, sharp dressers all, paying mock attention to the chatter of the far younger women. A few enlisted men and their girlfriends on the big splurge.

Lola stood weeping beside the hat-check stand. She was a curly brunette with porcelain skin and burgundy lipstick that overlapped the borders of her lips. A lacy tutu fringed her plump rear end. As Tom approached, she began to whimper. She and Mel had been sweet on each other until last week. She crooked her arm and threw a roundhouse punch at Tom's chin. He caught her wrist.

"Why'd you have to send Mel to the bank?" she moaned. "All the time you send Mel, why don't *you* go? You're the tough guy. You've got a gun. Mel

don't pack any kinda protection. He's a good boy."
She slapped her eyes with the heels of her hands
and whimpered again.

"Sorry," Tom muttered, and hustled out the
door then turned left on the sidewalk and double-
timed to the corner, where a crowd ringed the
action. He wedged and shoved his way through. The
medics were hoisting the cot into the ambulance. A
couple old women in long black coats stood bent
and wailing. As the ambulance pulled away, lights
out, the dozen or so rubbernecks dispersed, most of
them heading up C Street toward the roundup.

A pair of uniformed cops stayed behind. The
younger of them scribbled in a notepad while the
older cop, in a deep monotone, questioned a
witness. Apparently, the violence had given the
witness a case of jitters. He was a sailor in dress
whites who wrapped and unwrapped his cap from
around his index finger and kept shifting his weight
back and forth from one foot to the other. Even with
drab blond hair, a big head and a ruddy com-
plexion, he was handsome, rugged but graceful. He
looked like a college quarterback.

Tom leaned against the wall, eavesdropping. He
knew the cop. Ellison.

"We don't need your help, Tom," the cop said.

Tom pushed off the wall and stepped closer.
"All the same, it was my bartender got robbed and

112

killed. While delivering my money. Because I sent him. I'll stick around."

"Yeah, I heard you was a partner in Rudy's, along with that Jersey mobster. What's his name?"

"Paul Castillo."

"Say, maybe he knocked off your boy. Maybe he wants both halves of the loot."

Tom pointed to the sailor. "Get on with it, could you."

Ellison turned and rolled his hand for the kid to proceed with his story. The sailor talked carefully, measuring his words. "See, I'm just walking up to the newsstand to buy a pack of smokes and chewing gum, when out of the corner of my eye I glimpse this fella —" He pointed the direction the ambulance had gone. "He's rushing up the sidewalk like his pants are on fire. All of a sudden he stops cold. And ducks into this door-stoop." He jerked his thumb at the dark entryway a few feet to Hickey's right.

"I didn't hear nothing. Couldn't see. Ten, twenty seconds later, there's a shot then two more. Like the shooter wanted to make sure the guy couldn't squeal. And this Jap comes running out, got something tucked under his arm like a football. He beats it around the corner."

The young cop told the sailor to repeat. He did, in nearly the same words. A squad car pulled up across the street. A lab crew climbed out.

Tom double-timed back to Rudy's, dodged the headwaiter, the chef and the rest who wanted the story. Lola, he couldn't dodge. He allowed her to glare at him long enough to gather that he felt like hell, before he turned into his office and shut the door.

He scooped the keys out of his pocket, selected the little one and opened the upper right desk drawer. One of his rules to live by was — chase after a gunman, bring along a gun. Only the drawer was too light. He sifted under real estate documents and bank statements. No gun.

Lately, as partner in the supper club, with more private investigator work than he should've accepted, with his daughter growing into a young lady and his wife lodging regular complaints about his meager attentiveness and availability, he might have been pre-occupied enough to move the long-nosed .38 he had packed as an L.A. cop. Though he couldn't remember doing so, he might've taken the gun to the glove box of his car.

He rushed out, turned left through the kitchen, tripped on a mop handle, cussed and stumbled into the parking lot. The two reserved spaces closest to the door were empty. His and Castillo's. He whistled, called over the lot boy and demanded to know who had driven his car away. The boy swore the space had been empty when he came on duty at five. Before five, the lot was free, and nobody worked it.

Tom hustled back inside, to his office and rifled through every drawer. His spare keys — desk, business, home and car — were also missing. He stood a minute considering who might have burned him. One possibility eclipsed the rest. Besides his partner, the guy with most opportunity to open the desk was Fred Takahashi, the janitor until this morning, when he picked up his final check and tearfully said goodbye. Fred could easily have discovered the spare desk key on the hook behind the file cabinet. He had Rudy's to himself from three to nine a.m. every day but Tuesdays.

In case a fit of anger might flush away his guilt and sorrow, Tom kicked a beer can. He stomped out of the lot onto Third Street, turned the corner and strode past a young man pulling an old woman along toward the roundup while the woman screeched and tried to thrash out of his grip. He passed a trio of girls about his daughter's age, two of them Japanese, weeping in each other's arms. At the corner of Fourth and Broadway he climbed stairs, unlocked and opened a door whose lettering read: Hickey and Weiss, Investigations. From the upper right drawer of a weathered maple desk, he lifted a holster and a snub nosed .38 with a dusty rosewood grip. He wiped off the grip, checked the cylinders, removed his coat and strapped on the holster. He pocketed a handful of spare cartridges.

The roundup was on C Street between Tenth and Eleventh, out front of the YWCA. All the windows of the Y were lit. Residents leaned out gazing over the crowd. A few sat on the fire escape. A thousand or so milled in the street. The ones who talked used voices so bitter and painful Tom could read the emotions even if the sounds were foreign. Sudden high-pitched wails and screeches of outrage electrified the clammy air. Adults except the oldest stood while children gripped the mothers' legs or sat on blankets, suitcases or duffel bags. For all they knew, Tom was there to single them out and drag them off to execution. Even tough young men who normally swaggered recoiled at his approach, as he studied the faces searching for the generous mouth and high cheeks of Fred Takahashi.

"Mister Hickey. Mister Hickey!"

He spun and got clutched by a small, pale young woman with big eyes and ebony hair plaited into ropes. "Mister Hickey, is my brother at Rudy's?"

"Nope."

The girl was Fred's sister Janey, who used to make salads at Rudy's until she landed a better job, stocking airplane parts for Consolidated.

"Aw, doggone." She stared at his feet, rubbed her cheeks with both hands. "I'm getting awfully worried." She motioned for him to bend down close then whispered, "I can trust you, can't I?"

"Depends."

"What do you mean?"

"If Fred was the guy stole my gun and my car, robbed Mel on the way to the bank and shot him dead, I'm going to run him in."

She staggered backward and stood motionless except her eyes bulged and her head shook frantically even after Tom grasped her arm. He led her to a curb, helped her sit and sat beside her. He laid a gentle hand on the back of her neck, under the hair, turned her to face him and asked, "Why are you worried?"

She wagged her head, signaling Tom to let go. He did, and she shot a glance each direction, even above. "Until yesterday," she said, and paused a long while, her eyes closed and hands folded and wringing. Then she confessed, "Mister Hickey, he asked me to run away with him ... To Mexico. He swore he wouldn't let them lock him up ... Somebody killed Mel?"

"Yeah."

She bared her teeth as though to hiss. "Why do you blame Fred? Because he's Japanese?"

"Because somebody got into my desk, and a witness saw a Japanese guy running."

"Not my brother."

"Sure. Not Fred." He nodded until she appeared to believe him. "Look, give me a clue where to find him, or I have to go to the cops."

She wagged her head again, this time like thrashing.

"Now," he reached for her hand but stopped just short, "who do you think is more likely to shoot your brother on account of he's spooked, or just for the sport, the way things are tonight — me or your average lawman?"

She covered her face. Little moans issued from behind her hands. At last they played out. Then her voice came like a melody of peeps. "When I left the house, his suitcase was sitting by the door. I left him a note."

"What time?"

"About an hour ago."

The Takahashi place was on Irving Court, off Highland in National City. A Craftsman bungalow, the front porch spanned its width. In the back yard, dried corn stalks rustled. The family used to run a little truck farm, until the father died and his widow went to care for a sister in Kyoto, Japan. Fred and Janey tried to keep up the farm. Apparently they

118

had failed.

Tom watched through the rear window of a yellow cab parked on vacant lot behind a pepper tree. There was cloud cover and thick darkness, the only light spilling out of cracks between window shades and casements. The cabbie, named Mario, who claimed to have once been an opera singer, sat tugging on the ends of his mustache, clicking his tongue or combing his thick gray hair, while Tom watched, listened, entertained and cast out troublesome thoughts, about Fred as a hard working, congenial young man. Sympathy, he didn't need. Sympathy made a hunter of man or beast slow.

A light fog blew in. Tom was wiping his glasses when a crisp rustle issued from the corn. He tapped Mario on the arm, touched a finger to his own lips and listened. Nothing. He climbed out of the cab and tiptoed across the lot toward the rear of the Takahashi house and stationed himself at the edge of the lot, about twenty yards from the screened back porch, between two patches of dead tomato vines. Distant sirens droned. A neighbor laughed. Tires whirred along the nearby boulevards. He heard the clacking of a far off trolley and at last a thud like somebody jumping off the front porch onto a soggy lawn.

Tom bolted that way and got his foot tangled in a tomato vine. By the time he kicked free and reached the street, the person was starting down the hill fifty yards west. Tom sprinted to the hill, heard a motor racing then a screech and saw a black Chevy speeding away.

He sprinted back to the cab, jumped in and gasped, "Keep that Chevy in sight."

The whole West Coast was on blackout, awaiting another attack. A crescent moon and stars glowed feebly behind the ocean haze. In a taxi without headlights, Tom thought he might as well be chauffeured by a blind man. The cab fishtailed off the dirt onto the road, zoomed to the hill and down, clipped a hedge of oleanders making the left turn, reached Highland Boulevard in time to get stalled by a parade of dark cars chugging past a funereal speed.

"Lost him," Mario announced. "Give up?"

"You know any shortcuts to the border?"

"You bet. We can circle out east where nobody's going to object to the headlights."

"Step on it."

At a break in the procession, Mario swung left onto Highland. He caught Thirtieth and followed it to Sweetwater Road, poking behind the other dark shadows until the city limit when he switched on the headlights and roared around three cars.

They swooped down into Bonita Valley, swiveled between rolling hills, cut back onto Otay

Lakes Road and climbed a mesa while Tom attempted to reason. Would Fred actually try for the border, to pass through the gate when the border guards were bound to stop any Asian? Would he attempt to cross in a stolen car? Maybe. Desperate people aren't the shrewdest. Still, odds were Fred had other plans. Tom imagined loitering a couple hours at the border gate while the culprit, disguised as an old blind Eskimo woman with her dark glasses and seeing-eye dog, caught a flight to Anchorage.

He considered using the next payphone to report the stolen car and his suspicions to the law, though Janey had begged him not to. He hadn't made any promises, even when she pleaded for his word not to shoot her brother.

They sped on dirt and sand roads across the mesa about five miles without sighting another vehicle. The last leg of Mario's shortcut was a washboard trail through a cattle ranch. Here and there clouds parted and moonlight bathed the dingy shacks of vaqueros. A tractor bounded across a field, lights out. As they zoomed past a ranch house, a gunshot echoed off the hills behind them. Some patriot warning them to douse the lights and slow down. Mario said, "Mister, you pay damages."

He cut the lights as they approached Third Avenue, which led them through San Ysidro and on to the U.S. entry border compound, a gathering of shacks that looked like barracks hacked in two and boarded at the ends. Tom paid the fare and good tip. The cab spun a U turn and lined up with the three others heading back north, waiting to pick up a fare the Mexican saloons and gambling clubs hadn't clipped for his last dollar.

Tom adjusted his coat so the holstered gun wouldn't show. He strolled across the line, nodding casually to the U.S. border guard.

The guard at the Mexican station was a youngster in army fatigues, one of the special force the Mexican government had given Presidente Cârdenas to secure the frontier. Tom offered the boy his hand. The guard back-stepped.

In a mix of English and amateur Spanish, Tom explained that a pal had grabbed his car, as a prank. If the boy would simply allow him to hang out until a certain black '41 Chevy appeared and then engage the driver in a chat for about thirty seconds, he would find himself fifty dollars richer.

The boy scowled, perhaps while calculating that fifty dollars would equal two months pay. At last, he held out his hand.

Tom hadn't realized how commonplace was his car. At least one of every dozen vehicles was a black, '41 Chevy coupe. He watched the license plates. Peered at the drivers. Checked the right front fenders, since a drunk in Rudy's parking lot had flung open a car door and nicked his Chevy's glossy paint.

The guard watched him out of one eye and waited for a head-shake and wave before passing each black Chevy through. Over an hour and twenty minutes, six of them had crossed. None driven by an Asian. No Asian passengers.

The seventh had a license probably made by an imprisoned wise guy: IQ 065. It jolted to a stop, and Tom gave a quick, sharp whistle. When the guard looked over, he nodded. The driver was no Asian. He was a blond sailor in dress whites. His large head rested on a stubby neck. The witness to the robbery and murder. Driving a black, '41 Chevy. The plates, he had switched out. But he hadn't touched up the nick in the right front fender.

The guard approached the driver's window, his rifle pointed upward, the stock in the crook of his right arm, at ready to drop and fire. The sailor leaned out the window. The guard pitched questions rapid fire, while Tom used his key and his left hand to silently open the passenger door. He stepped onto the running board and slipped onto the seat. His right hand gripped the snub nosed .38.

The sailor heard the door click shut, spun half way around. "What the —?"

"*Buenos noches.* My Chevy handle's pretty well, doesn't she?"

A quick thinker, the sailor jerked around, back to face the window to enlist the border guard's help, only the Mexican had returned to his post beside the little shed. Already he was lighting a cigarette. The sailor squeezed the steering wheel and mumbled, "What're you, a hijacker?"

"Let's don't talk just yet. First, let's drive. Twenty five miles an hour, straight ahead, until I say different."

Last spring, a mother had viciously chastised her son for his licentious ways. A week later, she engaged Hickey to locate the kid, who had disappeared. Tom discovered that the son enjoyed Mexican girls and betting on cockfights at various ranchos along the border. But it was the Tijuana police who found him half buried in mud on a bank of the Tia Juana River, under the bridge about half way between the border and the downtown saloons. Apparently the kid had been on the bridge and dove, or fell, or got pushed.

As they crossed the bridge, Tom commanded the sailor to turn right at the far end, off the road onto a car path that led back around and under the bridge. When they hit the first large rut, something in the trunk that could be heavy luggage flew up and whacked the lid.

Tom commanded the sailor to park directly under the bridge. He used his free hand to dig the flashlight out of the glove box and shine it around. He spotted fire rings and other signs of encampments but no one in sight.

"What're we doing here?" the sailor stammered. "What's your game, mister?"

"Get out and spread eagle on the ground. Face down."

The sailor opened his mouth to argue. Tom stopped him with blow from the flashlight, a backhand to the upper lip and nose. Groaning, the sailor slowly reached for the door handle, opened the door and eased out, while Tom rounded the car. A motion of his head dropped the sailor, first to his knees then flat.

"Give me your billfold."

The sailor dug into his front pocket, laid the billfold on the dirt. Twenty-seven dollars and a Nevada driver's license in the name of Peter Rohn.

Tom reached into the car, plucked his keys out of the ignition and carried them around back. When the trunk sprang open, he caught the stowaway in his flashlight beam. "How's tricks, Fred."

Takahashi wept. His head wagged from shoulder to shoulder, slowly, as though to staunchly deny to the world and to himself that any of this nightmare was real. He climbed inch-by-inch out of the trunk.

"Get the suitcase," Tom said.

Fred pulled a small canvas satchel out of the trunk and dropped it at Tom's feet.

"Open it."

Tom rummaged through it, using his foot as a tool, and found mostly underwear. "Grab a few undershirts." He ordered Takahashi to use the shirts blindfolding the sailor and tying his own hands together, and then to blindfold himself. That done, Tom aimed the two men in the direction of the dirt mound that appeared to hold up the north end of the bridge. He shoved and commanded them to walk.

Both blindfolded men dragged their feet and stumbled. As they approached the hill, Tom commanded, "Hold it. Turn around. There we go. Now, before we proceed, let me clue you. A guy robs me, I might give him a break, as long as he squares things. The same guy lies, tries to make a fool out of me, he's a goner. Now, who'll talk first? Fred, you're on."

"Boss, when I gave him the keys, I made him promise to take your car back. It was supposed to be at Rudy's by closing time, so that you'd never know. Boss, I ...-"

"Hey," the sailor squawked. "He's giving you the business, can't you see? Here's the way it went — after the cops take my statement, see, I'm on the way back to my post, only I run into the lousy Jap here. I spot him sneaking into an alley down by Kettner, carrying the moneybag. I creep up behind him, catch him in a headlock, lift his rod and say I'm going to turn him in. But he wants to deal. Half the loot, he says, if I deliver him to TJ. That's all I done. Say, what's the gain for anybody if I turn him in? The dead guy's dead all the same."

Tom let silence fall and hang a while. To him, those moments felt strangely precious. Then a pariah dog trotted nearby and splashed into the knee-deep river.

Tom reached around Takahashi, loosed the blindfold and let it drop. He mimed shooting the gun into the air, pointed at Fred and then at the ground, a few times until the man's bewildered expression cleared and he nodded fervently.

Tom back-stepped and aimed at the hillside. As two reports echoed like ricochets off the bridge, Fred yowled, dropped to his knees and collapsed with a final groan.

"Hey! What?" the sailor wheezed.

"You want to say a quick prayer or talk straight?" Tom asked.

"Okay, okay," the sailor yelped. "The whole story, here it comes, take it easy. See, it was Lola, not me. Me and her were getting to be an item,and she's got a beef with this guy Mel, says he was stepping out on her. Well, one night, her and the Jap are copping a drink after closing time, and he's blabbing about his plan to ditch the roundup, get himself to Mexico. Lola comes out with, 'What say we swipe the boss's car. I'll get you to Mexico, bring the car back and nobody's the wiser.' So he lends her the office key, and when she's in there, she finds the gun and decides it might come in handy. She gives me the rod, says I oughta rob Mel and we can blow town before I ship out, on account of she knows I been dreaming about getting blown to smithereens over there. I ship out, I'm a goner. See, I got nothing to lose, everything to gain.

"Well, I'm wearing a bandana when I latch onto Mel and drag him into the door stoop, but he catches on. Recognizes my voice, I guess. Says my name and grabs for the gun. So I plug him. Wouldn't you? Self defense, mister. That's all. Besides, it was Lola's game, not mine. Hey, if it's the dough you're after, she's got it stashed."

Tom stood quietly shaking his head until Takahashi sat up and said, "Mel? Is Mel okay?"

"Beat it," Tom snapped. "Clear out, and don't let me see your mug, ever."

While Takahashi latched his suitcase and vanished into the pure darkness along the riverbed and the sailor stood cussing Lola and his own foolishness, Tom thought about the roundup.

Especially Janey.

And he thought about how easily a life could go to ruin.

Lola was wild and fickle, but hardly all bad. Just last week, she had sat in his office over a nightcap after closing, asked for his thoughts about love and family. Now, once he had turned the sailor over to San Diego cops at the border, he would go back to Rudy's and put the final touches on Lola's ruination.

He thought about the whole damned fragile world.

TOO SWEET

Alvaro Hickey had a wild streak. For three years, beginning at age five, he made his way as Tijuana street kid, living off theft and running errands for prostitutes.

Now, at seventeen, he had vanished without even telling his brother Clifford.

His adopted parents, Tom and Wendy Hickey, doubted he was gone for good. Still Wendy worried. Tom, a private investigator, promised to go hunting for the boy if he didn't show up in a week.

A Sunday evening in June, after Tom and Wendy had gone to bed, Clifford spotted his brother on television.

Clifford was watching the Steve Allen Show. During the part when Steverino led the audience out of the theater, across Vine Street, and up and down the aisles of the Hollywood Ranch Market, Alvaro brought up the end of the line. He was holding hands with Melody Sweet. But he didn't look happy as a guy ought to look holding hands with his first love who was now a celebrity.

Her real name was Melanie Sweedler. Sweet had been her mother's stage name. It fit Melanie. She had a voice so pure, even when she was in fourth grade, when Tom first heard her sing, even some of the rowdiest kids in the auditorium sat bug eyed or with their jaws gone slack. Seven years later, Tom still remembered her song, "Greensleeves," and the way Alvaro glowed with admiration. The boy had survived off his wit and charm. At eight years old, he'd been crafty and bold enough to pick the lock on the trunk of Tom's old Chevy, stow away and smuggle himself across the border. But sitting next to Melanie while they drove her home the night of that early performance, Alvaro looked as if a hangman had just slipped the noose on him. And he couldn't talk except in peeps.

Melanie's father had died long ago. She and her mom lived in one of the flimsy duplexes that had risen up on Grand Avenue in Pacific Beach during World War II. Her mom had done time as a Hollywood dancer and Vegas showgirl. Now she was a drunk who supported her habit with jobs like waitress and sales clerk. She rarely lasted a week. Their rent and food came from the V.A. pension Melanie's father earned them by crashing a Coast Guard helicopter during a rescue mission.

When his brother appeared on television, Clifford rushed to the door of his folks' bedroom. He knocked and opened it a crack. Wendy was sleeping

"It's Alvaro," Clifford said in an excited whisper. "On TV."

Tom jumped up and hurried to the living room, still wearing his glasses and holding a book on Chinese history. On the television, the line of tourists tagged behind Steve Allen. Tom and his son watched the procession file out past the coffee and hamburger bar where a trio of would-be starlets wiggled and beamed and a teenaged boy and girl who slumped against the counter gave the camera their James Dean sneers. Tom and Clifford watched until the last of the tourists had crossed Vine and gone into the theater. No Alvaro.

"Okay Pop," Clifford said, "I'm not on drugs, I'm not hallucinating. They were there."

Tom nodded.

Clifford stared at him for a minute and said, "I'm going with you."

"Nope."

"Look —"

"We don't leave your mother alone, right?"

"Yeah but —"

"And who's got school?"

"Me but —"

"And who's the family bloodhound?"

Tom caught a few hours sleep. By dawn, he was racing through San Clemente, trying to keep his foot still when it wanted to floor the pedal. Tom loved driving, the faster the better. One reason he treasured the ten-year-old Chevy wagon was, police aren't as likely to chase and ticket a faded green four-door.

He slipped off his shoe so his accelerator foot wouldn't be quite as heavy. He tuned the radio to the first L.A. jazz station he could find. Brubeck, Monk, Ramsey Lewis and Jao Gilberto accompanied him past orange groves and Disneyland and into the city, while he thought about Melanie. Mostly about her breakdown three years ago.

He didn't know all the facts. He knew that Melanie's mom and some boyfriend of hers had got into a spat. The boyfriend landed in Emergency with a kitchen knife in his belly, but he wouldn't press charges. And the judge looked unkindly upon woman-beaters, which kept Brenda Sweedler out of jail and Melanie out of the foster home Tom and Wendy would have offered.

Melanie cracked up at school, during eighth grade English class. She was a model student. She loved books and all kinds of art and pleasing her teachers, but after the fight in her apartment, nerves over-powered her brain and will. During that spell, when Alvaro walked her home or through the halls, she might say a few words but never could finish a sentence. A month passed, then the teacher asked her to present her report on *Great Expectations*. Instead of admitting she hadn't

133

finished, she collapsed. She slipped from her seat, fell to the floor and wept, wailing and thrashing around while Alvaro knelt beside her and pushed desks, chairs and people out of the way until the school nurse and her aide came. They picked Melanie up and led her off.

After six weeks in a county mental health facility, she returned home and to school. But she wouldn't sing anymore, or read aloud, or even stand with a group in front of the class for a spelling bee.

So, three years later, after Melanie once again sang, now accompanied by Paul Case on guitar, in a talent program at Pacific Beach High School, people considered Case a miracle worker.

He taught junior English, American Literature. The girls in his classes worshipped him. After all, he moonlighted as a folksinger and had cut a record with a trio called The Wanderers. And the shaggy hair and beach boy tan helped him look younger than his thirty-some years.

Tom exited on Firestone and pulled into a Richfield station next to a diner where long ago he and other L.A. police officers used to meet for coffee. A Mexican fellow was on the pay phone. When he saw Tom approaching, he hung up and hustled away, perhaps wary of a guy in a sport coat, hand-painted tie and fedora.

At 7:30, Tom called a number for Melanie he had found in Alvaro's desk. After many rings he gave up and called Brenda Sweedler's number. He let the phone ring about fifteen times.

"What?" she yawned into the receiver.

"We saw Mel on TV last night. Steve Allen."

"Big deal. She's on TV at least once a week. This Tom Hickey or who?"

"It's Tom. Alvaro was with her."

"So what?"

"I told you a week ago, he ran off."

"Oh, yeah, well now you got him."

"First I need Melanie's address."

The boarding house was on Selma near Gower, mid-way up a block of bungalows shaded in poplar and eucalyptus, in a mansion that looked like it came from Pasadena, with the Spanish tile and balconies.

On one of the balconies a pretty blonde stood, leaning on the rail. She smiled and waved to Tom as if he had come to serenade her.

A sign above the archway read, "Maude Sinclair's Home for Ladies." When Tom was a boy in Hollywood, he saw plenty of those places, meant as sanctuaries, where the girls who migrated from Iowa and Kansas to become starlets often made their first stop, part because they feared the local wolves, part to comfort their worried moms and dads.

He passed beneath the archway and into a courtyard that featured tall agave and pillars of bougainvillea climbing the walls. He hadn't yet passed the cactus garden on his way to the stairs that led to the second floor rooms when a high voice trilled, "Mister, oh Mister."

When he turned, he saw a buxom woman of around his own age, sixty years. She had a pale face except the splotches of rouge, and yellow hair in tight curls. Her long, blousy skirt was the same yellow.

He greeted her, introduced himself and said, "Melanie Sweedler will want to see me."

"Be that as it may," Maude Sinclair told him, "no men are allowed in the ladies' rooms. I'll go myself and ask if in fact she does care to see you."

She strode to the staircase and limped up, using the side rail. At the top, she rested then turned right toward the street-facing rooms, went to the third door, and rapped on it. After a minute or so, she knocked again, and waited before she turned and came back.

Tom met her at the foot of the staircase. She gave him a look of dark chagrin. He asked, "You think she didn't come home last night?"

"If she didn't, I'm not surprised. She's the flighty, wayward sort."

Though the Melanie Tom knew was reserved, cautious to a fault, and always respectful of authority and rules, he nodded and listened for more.

"She drinks, I'm rather certain, although I haven't yet put my hands on her liquor."

Which meant, Tom thought, the woman had used her key and gone snooping. "But you're certain she drinks. How's that?"

"I see it in her eyes and in the rubbery way she walks. I hear it when she speaks, just the hint of a slur."

"How about men?"

Sinclair looked as if he'd made her bite a lemon. "I caught her trying to sneak that folksinger into her room."

"Folksinger, you say?"

"The one who struts around behind his big guitar, on that silly 'Hoot and Holler' show."

"You know him?"

She was staring at his tie. "Are you a policeman?"

"A friend of the family."

Sinclair staged an expression of woe. "The girl told me she has no father. What a trial such a rebel must have been to her poor mother."

"The man," Tom said. "Paul Case, correct?"

"If that's the name of the leader and elder of that troupe of hers. The one who drives a brand new Lamborgini."

"Any other men?" Tom asked.

She placed a finger to her mouth as though to assure him gossip was beneath her. "Not three days ago, I happened upon her on this very path brazenly holding hands with a Mexican boy. They were going to her room. Oh, I'll admit he was handsome. Still, I believe that shows how far she's fallen."

Tom nodded. "Two men. Any others?"

"Not that I saw, but surely an older man and a Mexican are two too many."

"How about girlfriends?" Tom gestured toward rooms that surrounded the courtyard.

She held up both hands as though to stop him from disturbing any of her ladies. "I believe she's too busy with her troupe, her men, and gadding about. Still, I shall inquire. You may call me at this number." She pulled a card out of a pocket in the folds of her skirt.

Tom shook her hand and walked past the cactus garden and out of the courtyard. He meant to move his station wagon farther down the block, watch for and intercept Melanie or any of Maude Sinclair's girls on their way into or out of the home through the archway, the only passage to the courtyard. But the blonde was still on her balcony.

She gave him a droopy grin. "Hi'ya handsome. Ol' Maudey give you the boot?"

He smiled. "Yes ma'am." Then he risked Sinclair's wrath by crossing her lawn to stand beneath the blonde's balcony. "I'll bet you're a friend of Melanie's."

"You bet right. Who are you?"

"Tom Hickey."

"Hickey, you say." She leaned so far toward him, to study his face, Tom got ready to break her fall. "Like Melly's dreamboat. Only you don't look like him."

"He's my son. I need a word with him. Help me out, would you?"

"What day's this?"

"Monday."

"Okay, right. Let's see, is it Monday mornings The Wanderers record? Yeah, it is."

Paul Case had recruited a dozen singers, including a few guitar strummers. They were mostly kids. Melanie, Tom believed, was the youngest. Case promoted them around the L.A. folk clubs and landed them a spot on a weekly variety show called "Hoot and Holler," which won them a contract with Capitol. If they were recording today, it would be in the Capitol Building, an eyesore that looked like a dozen dinner plates stacked upside down, a block up the hill from Hollywood and Vine. He parked curbside across Vine and fed the meter. If he'd been looking for Melanie, he might've gone to the Capitol front desk and asked for admission to the studio. But he was looking for Alvaro, who could be loitering anywhere in the neighborhood, waiting for her session to finish, or running errands, coming and going to fetch the group's cough drops and sodas.

So he sat in his wagon and thought about Melanie. Maybe the Sinclair woman was right and Melanie had turned her problems over to liquor, like her mother. And like her father, from what Tom had heard about the man. Tom supposed Melanie could've been nipping at her mama's sauce since she was a baby, and caught the habit that way. But he still couldn't feature Melanie as a drunk. Of all the drunks he'd known, which were a legion, none had been so guarded or self-controlled as Melanie. As a sometime jazz musician, Tom had known more than his share of guys and gals who reminded him of Melanie. Gifted introverts. The kind most likely to become junkies.

His Timex read 11:15, and he was thinking about a sandwich, when he spotted his son on a bus stop bench down the hill past Hollywood. He

crushed the fire in his pipe with a golf tee he kept
for that purpose and left the pipe in the ashtray. He
jumped out of the car. While he walked, he watched
Alvaro cross Vine and go a few steps east then stop
and stand still looking down at the sidewalk. He
stood there the whole time Tom waited for the light
at Hollywood Boulevard to change, and while he
crossed the street.

When Tom reached him, the boy was still gazing
down, at the star that commemorated Mary Pick-
ford, an actress Tom's mother had worked for and
about whom he'd told his boys a few stories.

He said, "She was one of the good ones."

Alvaro looked up, with a weary and mirthless
smile. "Let's see. I'm on TV last night, you find me
this morning. About twelve hours. Not bad."

Tom hung his arm across the boy's shoulders.
"You didn't tell us where you were going
because...?"

"See, at first, when Mel called, I figured I'd just
come up for the day. Then, you know."

"Nope," Tom said. "I sure don't."

Alvaro pointed across the Boulevard. "Here they
come."

A gang of young folks had poured out of the
Capitol Building. All but two of them walked down
Vine, and as they came closer Tom recognized the
bunch he had watched every Thursday for the six

or eight weeks since they landed the TV spot. They looked wholesome, fresh, unlike most folk singers. Tom had no passion for blazing banjos, the strums of relentless guitars, or for any kind of foot stomping number except those of gospel choirs. But Melanie's every song threatened to break his heart. Last week she soloed on "Barbara Allen," a ballad about a dear girl who dies from shame and lost love. For the first time in maybe thirty years, a tear had dribbled out from the corner of his eye.

With some hugs, backslaps and victory waves, the group dispersed in three directions. Paul Case and Melanie stepped into the crosswalk at Hollywood and Vine at the same time a guy in jeans and an L.A. Angels ball cap ambled up behind Paul Case. Tom didn't see him pull the gun.

They were halfway across Vine. A second after what could sound to the untrained like a distant backfire, Case lurched forward and staggered, leading with his head, toward the curb in front of the Taft Building. He touched down a few yards from Tom, his head ramming straight into the ridge of the curb.

Tom should've kept his eye on the shooter. But he didn't. He couldn't pull his eyes off Melanie, who had stopped cold in the middle of Vine and stood long enough for Alvaro to dash to her. Then she collapsed into Alvaro's arms.

An hour later, no detective had shown up. Still, the young patrolmen, when they finished jotting notes, let the Hickeys and Melanie and most of the surviving Wanderers go on their way.

Wedged between Tom and son in the front seat of the Chevy, Melanie quaked. Her wavy, honey brown hair rippled. Her sobs were like gasps so deep they choked her and made her gasp again for air. They turned her pale cheeks to crimson.

"At least she's not so gone as that time in eighth grade," Alvaro said.

"Is she using?"

Alvaro turned away, toward the hills. For a minute, he kept her secret. "Yeah, but not like you think, not off the street. Pills, capsules actually. Sometimes, like before a show, when she needs a real jolt to stay cool, she pours it out of the capsule and snorts it."

"Morphine?"

"I guess. Melanie doesn't even know. They just give it to her."

"Who's they?"

"Whoever's on duty at this place we're taking her to."

As they turned onto Primrose, a half mile up from Cahuenga, Alvaro said, "Dad, who do you think shot that Case?"

"A pro, for sure. One shot, with a silencer, top of the spine, then disappears."

"I wonder why."

"The music business is dirty," Tom said.

Alvaro nodded and started petting Melanie's hair. "So's the dope business."

The clinic was a '30s mansion Tom remembered well as the playhouse of Eleanor Boone, a silent movie vamp. Her favorite seamstress was Tom's mother, who would come home from fittings and rant at Tom and his sister about all the boozing and fornication that went on at Eleanor's house.

Melanie took a few steps on her own while Tom and Alvaro lifted and bolstered her between them, taking her into the clinic. She felt bone thin, seemed to weigh nothing.

Whoever owned the clinic must be an Eleanor Boone fan, Tom thought. The place was a ringer for the one in his memory. With it's murals of mythical goat-men chasing plump wood nymphs, the decor seemed more likely to drive patients mad than help heal them.

On the wall behind the ebony desk hung a layout of at least a dozen photos in gilded frames. Each of them featured a famous actor, actress, politician or athlete standing or sitting beside the same fellow, a guy who made Orson Welles look gentle and trim.

144

A girl in a short-skirt nurse outfit came around from behind the desk. Her nametag read "Lilly." She had skinny legs and smeared cherry lipstick. She rushed to open a door, which the men helped Melanie through, into a room of burgundy leather couches and a single well-padded executive's chair. When they seated her on one of the couches, she quit sobbing long enough to gaze around. And she gave Tom a look he believed meant "Save me."

So he kissed her cheek and said to Alvaro, "Call your brother. If I don't get back here by, say, suppertime, we'll use him to relay messages. Tell him that."

"You don't need my help, Pop?"

"Not like Melanie does. But, yeah." He looked to make sure the girl in the nurse outfit had left. "Snoop around. Find out all you can about this place."

Alvaro nodded. "Pop, Mel's no junkie. It's just, she hadn't hardly sung ever since eighth grade. And Paul Case, he knew the key, he had the stuff. Mel still thinks he set her free."

Tom reached out and squeezed his son's shoulder then let go and started to leave. But he stopped and turned back. "Mel called you every week or so. What made you come up this time?"

"She was crying, and spooked. Paul Case was acting scary, she said. Like Brett, remember him?

The guy her mom stabbed. And he'd snatched a bottle of her pills, she told me when I got up here. But a couple days later, before she ran out of her stuff, he gave her two bottles. And he didn't look scary to me."

In the lobby, Tom leaned on Lilly the nurse's big desk.

"She'll be just fine," the girl said.

"Who's the boss here?" Tom asked. "That guy all over the wall?" He pointed to the layout of photos.

"Doctor Worth. He owns the building and everything," she said, sounding impressed as if her employer owned California.

"I need to talk to Doctor Worth. Soon."

She reached for an appointment ledger and found the right page. "Perhaps Friday at four p.m. will work for you."

"Perhaps not. Where is he now?"

"He's in Las Vegas," she said, as if that chintzy town were Paris.

"That'll do," he said. "Which hotel?"

Tom only left Melanie in that place because the very sight of it had calmed her, and now wasn't the time for her to kick any habits.

He found a payphone outside a newsstand on Cahuenga. Twenty-five years after he left the LAPD, not many of his pals were still cops. But a switchboard operator helped by reading names off her roster. She connected him to Pete Battaglia. He only remembered Pete as a rookie in uniform. Now he ran a detective team in homicide.

The Paul Case murder had gone elsewhere but Pete had heard talk about it.

"Who's got it?" Tom asked.

"Let's see ... That'd be Gonzo. Gonzales to you."

"Say, Pete, what do you know about one Doctor Worth, psychiatrist, has a clinic on Primrose?"

"Just he's been known to produce a few movies, or so say the gossips."

"Movies, huh?"

"Nothing that's going to win him an Oscar," Battaglia said. "The kind you don't want to send your kids to. Why? Paul Case into the Doctor for something?"

"You tell me."

"I got my own challenges, Tom. Talk to Gonzo."

It was Tom's first trip to the City Hall, new since his L.A. years, that towered above its surroundings like some gothic cathedral in the plaza of a humble village.

He located Gonzales on the third floor in a long, narrow room crammed with matching gray desks that reminded Tom of a nightmare after reading

Franz Kafka. To the rookie who stood up and greeted him, he said, "Tell Lieutenant Gonzales I can describe the Paul Case murderer, would you?"

The rookie fetched his lieutenant from an office sectioned out of the back corner of the room. Gonzales was young for a lieutenant and either a frequent fighter or not much of one, judging from his flat, bent nose.

Tom spent a minute describing the scene and the shooter. Gonzales set his note pad on the nearest desk and folded his arms. "How old are you?"

"Old enough." Tom said.

"Well, in all that time nobody told you to stick around a crime scene until a detective arrives, tell *him* what you saw?"

"What do you think?" Tom asked. "Music or dope?"

"Dope, you say?"

"Just a thought."

Gonzales unfolded his arms. "Dig a little." He rolled his hand. "Just where did that thought come from?"

Tom shrugged. "Say I stumble across a dope pusher with M.D. after his name, who do I deliver him to?"

"How about you give me the name and we do the stumbling?"

"There's an idea," Tom said, as he turned away, toward the elevator.

Tom preferred to drive fast especially when he was mad or more fed up with the world than usual. His favorite drive was the road to Las Vegas, the part beyond the state line. In Nevada, the only speed law was, don't crash into anything. His Chevrolet station wagon hadn't the muscle or weight of the Cadillac he'd long threatened to buy, but it ran the big motor, a 350 cubic inch V-8. The tires were new, the front-end steady.

He got stalled by an overturned semi in Pomona. He rolled up the windows and smoked his pipe all through the San Bernardino Valley, preferring to gag on smog of his own making. Once on the open highway, he only managed to drive within ten m.p.h. of the speed limit by telling himself he could make up for the aggravation once he reached Nevada. He pulled through the Bun Boy in Baker for a couple hamburgers with plenty of soggy bread and bite sized patties of meat he didn't want much of anyway.

He crossed the state line at 4:10 p.m., did the fifty miles left into Vegas, and checked into the Desert Inn all before 5:00.

On a hunch, he started at the pool and got lucky. He found Doctor Worth, greased and brown and lying on his back in a chaise-lounge. His fingers tapped like a frantic pianist's on his medicine ball belly.

Tom sat across the pool, ordered a Dewar's from the leggy bar runner. He tipped her big and got an inviting smile.

Doctor Worth couldn't lie still. Every minute or so, he hoisted his bulk up with his elbows and looked both ways and as far around back as his beefy neck would allow. The temp had to be a hundred plus even after six p.m. And fat guys could sweat for no reason. Even so, the sweat pouring off him looked excessive. The drinks he bought were tall and icy and looked like Tom Collins's. They gave him something else besides his belly to drum his fingers on.

Tom knew from the photos in the clinic that Worth could look imposing, tough as a gorilla, in the right outfit. But neither his swimsuit nor his fright flattered him. Today he looked half as menacing as Pooh Bear.

The last wedge of sun dipped behind the far mountains. Doctor Worth picked up his towel and yellow and orange Hawaiian shirt and padded on small feet and short legs to the sliding door of a room that opened onto the lawn that bordered the pool deck.

Tom counted the rooms from the end of the wing

to the one Worth had gone into. He strolled to the end of the wing, entered the interior corridor, and walked the length of it, counting doors until he reached the doctor's.

From a comfortable chair in the lobby, he kept an eye on the door to Suite 118. When a bellhop passed, he requested a phone and tipped the bellhop well. The fellow whispered, "You don't know who to call, I could give you some numbers."

Tom shook his head and phoned home. When Clifford answered, Tom apologized for taking so long to check in.

Clifford said, "Alvaro's called four times already."

"Is Melanie okay?"

"She still isn't talking, but she's not shaking so bad. He said to tell you he's monitoring the dosage. When did he get to be a medic?"

"I'd rather not ask."

"Yeah, and he said to tell you some nurse called Lilly flipped out when he told her about Paul Case getting shot. She was blubbering when Alvaro called me one time and still blubbering the next time he called. She told him Case was her first boyfriend, and they made some movie together."

"Pop, Alvaro's as worried about you as he is about Melanie. He says you're chasing a murderer."

Tom said, "I leave murderers to the police these days."

"Where are you, anyway?"

"Vegas. The Desert Inn. My room's 167, but I'm in the lobby now."

"Why'd you go there?"

"It's Lilly's boss's favorite hideaway. Lilly likes to talk. Listen, If your mama asks, just tell her I'm fine and due home tomorrow, maybe by afternoon. Clifford, you and Alvaro will need to share a bedroom for a while. Make your room or Alvaro's up for Melanie, would you?"

"No, how about I let her sleep in with me. I mean, I'll sleep on the floor, promise."

"I guess a son like you is what I get for being a wise guy."

"Hey, Pop ... don't get shot or anything. Okay?"

"I'll see you tomorrow."

A room service cart that passed by Tom and made him salivate with its broiled steak smell continued on to room 118. When the cart was on its way back, he stopped the waiter and asked for a steak sandwich and a Dewar's.

"To what room, sir?" the waiter asked.

"Just bring it back here, I'll take it out by the pool."

When the meal came, he ate it in the lobby and stepped outside for a smoke in a place where he could watch Room 118 through the glass doors. He had finished all but the pickle when Doctor Worth lumbered out of his room.

He wore white slacks and a red and blue Hawaiian shirt. His moist face glistened. Tom backed around a corner, suspecting the doctor would pass him on his way to the parking lot. When he didn't, Tom went back to the lobby and saw the man halfway down the wing that led to the casino.

Worth lumbered straight to a cashier window, where he scribbled on a house check or an I.O.U. He carried his new stack of chips to the closest roulette table. Minimum bet $10.

Tom wasn't much of a gambler, but he'd spent a couple years as Chief of Security at Harry's Casino in South Lake Tahoe, so he knew losing bets when he saw them. Every spin, the doctor would lay a stack on a single number and make a play of covering the long shot with another stack on black or red. He kept repeating the bet on different numbers and different colors, and hardly paid attention to the ball or where it landed.

When his chips ran out, he returned to the cashier, all the time shooting glances right and left and over his shoulders.

He lost another stack of chips on baccarat, came back to the cashier for more then settled at a blackjack table, $20 minimum, across an aisle from the table where Tom sat watching and playing dime

153

Keno. For a while, luck overthrew the doctor's carelessness, and he gathered a mountain of chips. But he either didn't notice or care when a mechanic with giant paws and sunglasses came in as relief for the dealer, though anybody half-wise to casinos would know he was there to sneak looks at the second card, toss whichever of the two suited him, and break the winner's spell. Four players knew, and left the doctor and a diamond-studded older woman to get robbed.

Shortly after midnight, the doctor's chips ran out once again. He started back toward the cashier, shooting glances everywhere, but veered off and tottered toward a dark place with tables and bar and food service. When a girl in a tutu tapped the doctor on his shoulder and he leaped a yard off his chair, Hickey decided he'd seen enough.

As he neared, the doctor's small white hands flew up and clutched the edge of the table. Hickey nodded and sat down. "What's up, Doc?"

Worth's cheeks became balloons. "Huh," he said, as all the breath he'd held spewed out.

To get the doctor's reaction, Tom said, "Say, is Paul Case the first guy you've had killed?"

The doctor let out a frail squeal and started to rise. But when Hickey touched his side where a gun might've been if he'd worn one, the man sank back into his chair and began to quiver. "I don't know

154

anything about —

"Shh. Let's take it out by the pool."

While they walked down the wing toward the lobby with Tom steadying him like he would steady a blind drunk, the doctor asked three times, "What are we doing?"

Tom didn't answer. He was thinking how he'd changed over a lifetime. Once, the thought of what he meant to do now, play by instinct rather than rules, would've horrified his sense of justice. In the old days, he'd thought the civilized world needed guys like him to uphold its principles. Anymore, he left rulebooks and civil justice to the young.

The doctor said, "You're not a cop, are you?"

Tom didn't bother to answer. Worth didn't seem to notice or care that urine dribbled out of his pant leg and onto the floor while Tom led him through the hotel lobby and out to the pool deck and parked him on a lounge chair poolside. On the far deck, a couple smooched between giggles and coos.

"Did they send you to kill me?" the doctor whimpered.

"They?"

"Well, Rusty ... Paul's agent, I guess?"

"Never mind that," Tom said. "I might not kill you if you'll do me a little favor."

The relief on the fat man's face made Tom want to kick him into the pool, dive in behind and drown him.

"A favor?"

"We take a ride," Tom said. "We go to L.A., you talk to Lieutenant Gonzales, tell him how you prescribed a little girl who never had a physical pain in her life all the morphine she could swallow. That's it. You find a new occupation. I go away. Deal?"

The doctor had fallen to panting so hard, Hickey needed to slap him. Which he enjoyed.

"How about it?" Tom said.

"Yeah, sure," the doctor stammered. "Sure, it's a deal."

Standing beside his Chevy, Tom said, "You're not getting into my wagon soaked in piss." He pointed to the doctor's white trousers. "Take those off."

Worth unzipped, unsnapped and let them fall and stepped out of them, all the while watching Tom's hands.

"Those too." Tom pointed at the man's silk boxer shorts.

The doctor's mouth opened but snapped shut as he glanced up at Tom's face. He peeled the shorts down and stepped out of them, already trying to cover his privates with his small hands.

Tom opened the trunk, grabbed a blanket and threw it at Worth. "Get in back."

The doctor left his clothes on the asphalt and climbed in. Tom slid behind the wheel then reached over and opened the glove box. The pistol he pulled out, he showed to the doctor before laying it on his lap.

The aging Chevy wagon behaved like a family car until they left the strip for the highway and passed the city limits. Then it roared into the desert.

After a few miles, Worth yelled over the hot wind through the open front windows. "Paul Case was going to kill me.

Tom rolled up the windows. "Let me guess. You saved Case from going to the streets for his fix. He paid you by playing the stud in a movie or two. When he struck it rich, you offered to sell him the prints. Fair enough. But he disagreed and threatened you."

The doctor's silence backed up Tom's speculation.

After a long minute Worth mumbled, "Who told you those lies?"

"Hush," Tom said. He switched hands on the wheel, grabbed the .38 off his lap, threw his arm around and aimed the pistol at Worth's head. "Sit still and keep quiet, Doc. Let me forget you're still alive."

The speedometer hand bounced between 110 and 120. Feeling a slight pull to the left, Tom wondered if he needed a wheel alignment. And he wondered how much this exploiter of the troubled and the too sweet to survive in a crass and violent world could handle. How much fright would it take before the fat man's heart caved in?

Worth had lifted the blanket to shield his sweaty face from the wind through the open windows. A truck blasted by going east. A little squeal issued out of him.

They were almost to the state line when he peeped, "Could we *please* slow down?"

Tom jammed the accelerator so hard he thought he might've dented the floorboard.

Marcelino Contreras threw a party to celebrate the engagement of his daughter Elena to Alvaro Hickey.

The Contreras home was grand. Elena gave tours to cousins and other guests. She spent most of each tour in the gallery where Marcelino exhibited his surrealist treasures. The highlights were a painting and four lithographs by Juan Miro, worth enough to buy a block of homes in Alvaro's neighborhood.

The home loomed a quarter mile uphill from the Point Loma yacht club. On the balcony, Alvaro stood watching sails ripple while sunset gilded the harbor. It ricocheted off the Navy's armada docked at North Island, darkened the low mesa that rose from the Pacific, climbed past the eastern outskirts of Tijuana and on until it reached the mountains.

He was gazing at a lone dark cloud that appeared to rest atop Mount San Miguel when Marcelino came and laid an arm across his shoulder. "*Que bonito*, isn't it?"

Alvaro nodded.

"San Diego." Marcelino said, looking proud as if he owned the city. "*Mira, mi hijo*. I've been thinking about you."

"Oh."

"Yes. And I have concluded that you are destined for greatness."

Alvaro laughed. "Elena told you I went four-for-four the other day?"

With just the hint of a smile, Marcelino said, "I'm afraid you are too old to begin a career in baseball. However, you are smart, handsome, well spoken, passionate."

Alvaro put up his guard.

"And you have a heart for the people. No?"

"Most people, sure."

"I can see you are thinking, what's this *hombre* leading up to?"

Alvaro nodded.

"What it is, is this. You were born to become a leader, a *politico*."

A fellow like Marcelino, kind enough and generous but at least mildly infected with arrogance, you couldn't rush without offending. For the next few hours he alternated between hosting and returning to Alvaro. Each time he delivered more of his plan to run Alvaro for District Attorney, as a rung on the ladder toward higher places. His strategy was already populated with details about the campaign. He meant to make his son-in-law into one of the

160

rulers. A crowd Alvaro distrusted more than any.

Most of the night Alvaro brooded. Besides his
distrust of the powerful, he wondered how political
power might change him. He questioned
Marcelino's motives, and what the fellow might ask
of someone he made. And he questioned what
would become of the marriage, and of Elena, should
he decline.

He might've slept three hours. Then, after coffee
and a shower failed to disperse the mind-fog, he
went to the phone. He meant to call Tom Hickey,
his father by adoption. He was at his desk, in the
guest room office of his duplex, staring at the
guitar-shaped phone Elena had given him. It rang.

"*Mi hijo*," a woman said.

He didn't recognize the voice, even though she
called him son, like Marcelino had last evening.
Elena's mother? he wondered. Then his heart
jumped and stuck in his throat. Because, he
imagined, this could truly be his mother, if what his
papa had claimed, and what he'd believed for thirty
years, that she had gotten snatched away and
murdered by agents of the Mexican government,
was dead wrong.

"You don't know me?" she said.

Now he recognized the voice, though it sounded
a century older than last time, only months ago.

"*Lo siento, mi tia,*" he said. "*Estoy preoccupado.*"

"Come to my house right away."

Of all the women Alvaro had known, he might've voted Angelina the toughest. A fragile woman didn't survive fifteen years as a Tijuana prostitute. But today she sounded as if she were dying.

She lived in San Ysidro, a block off the main boulevard and across Pepper Drive from the library. Her bungalow was the third on the east in a court of green plastered studios.

Before he finished his knock, she commanded him to enter.

The curtains to the front and rear windows were drawn shut. The only light came through the bathroom's mottled glass window.

The place smelled of dirty laundry and mildew. Otherwise, it could've passed for an acquisitive nun's prayer room. Every visit, Alvaro noticed more *ritablos*, miniature portraits on tin usually painted by the unskilled, to commemorate some received or desired blessing or miracle. They hung on every wall, and perched on the corner table, the dresser, and the bookshelf.

Angelina wore a maple brown housedress, a shade lighter than her face and arms. She was sitting on a wooden dining chair, her back straight, her face set like stucco.

162

He stared, considered, then attempted a light remark. "What'd I do?"

Her face only darkened. Her right hand rose and drifted to the white folding table beside her. It landed beside the pistol. A black Smith and Wesson 9mm.

"What's that for?" Alvaro said.

She crooked her face toward the weapon. "I was going to shoot myself. God told me not to."

On the far side of the gun lay a section of newspaper, rolled as if to swat flies. She reached over the gun and brushed the paper off the table in Alvaro's direction. It lit on the threadbare carpet beside her bare foot.

He supposed she intended for him to pick it up. Instead, he crossed the room, leaned over and kissed her forehead. Her flesh was crusted in powder, as if for days she had caked layer upon layer.

He back-stepped and picked up the newspaper then moved a sewing basket off the only other chair in the place and sat down. He unrolled the paper and squinted to make out the words.

The top headline translated, LUZ CARTEL IMPLICATED IN ENSENADA MASSACRE.

Alvaro knew the story. Last week, in what appeared to be a feud between drug gangs, gunmen had entered the home of cartel boss Fidel Orca and opened fire. They shot and killed Orca's wife, his mother, two of his sisters, a niece and two nephews, his grandfather and grandmother. His four children, a gardener and two maids, they hacked and shredded with the gardener's machete.

Alvaro looked up and mumbled, "Christ, not J.P.?"

Her hands folded in her lap. Her eyes pinched closed.

"How do you know it was J.P.?" he demanded.

"I know. I know people who know these things."

"Not maybe? For sure?"

Her eyes snapped open and shot poison at him. "I know," she shouted. "I know everything my son does."

Alvaro leaned back, stared at a *ritablo*, a blue-eyed, haloed angel with one healthy and one broken wing. "Okay. So would you like to come stay with me until you get through this?"

"No." Her voice had gone gentle, as though she were addressing a lover or a saint. "I want you to do something. I want you to go to Juan Pedro."

Alvaro nodded. He turned away and shuffled across the room and back while searching for a way to tell her what she must already know. He knelt beside her, lay his hand atop her folded hands. "*Tia*, if you want me to convince J.P. to quit working for Luz, it's not like that. He's gone way beyond the quitting point."

She didn't budge, or breathe. Her hands got colder. "I don't want you to talk to Juan Pedro. I want you to kill him."

A quarter mile short of the border gate, Alvaro parked in the lot in front of Denny's. He went inside, sipped coffee, nibbled steak and scrambled eggs, and thought about Elena, Pop, his brother Clifford, and Clifford's kids. Strange, he reflected, that while contemplating murder he found himself more worried about what the people he loved would think of him than about right or wrong, whether J.P. would kill him, or if he would end his life in prison, like his papa had.

He knew what Elena would think. Even the knowledge that he'd considered killing would horrify her. Even for that, she might leave him. He wouldn't blame her. What he loved most about Elena was her innocence, though he supposed it was a product of the sheltered life Marcelino gave her. Apparently the privilege that spoiled so many enlarged the purity of a few. In the year they had dated, he'd seen no hint of conceit or any attitude of superiority or entitlement. She was wise enough to recognize her blessings. The idea of wounding her innocence by turning her man into a murderer wrenched Alvaro's insides from brain to bowels.

How Pop and Clifford would react, he could only guess. Either of them might try to tackle and clap him into a straight jacket before they let him even go to J.P. They knew J.P ran with the Luz mob, who not only killed rivals, but also police chiefs, reporters, honest politicos. Anyone who posed a threat. Including childhood amigos, he imagined.

He thought of leaving his Camaro in the Denny's lot, crossing the line on foot and taking a cab to Baby Love. But should he decide to kill J.P., the only way he could do so and escape was to get J.P. into his car.

On the road to Baby Love, he wondered what led him to even consider this madness. He thought back and believed he would've walked out on Angelina if she hadn't promised to kill herself rather than live anymore knowing her sins had turned a monster loose on the world. Even so, he might've walked out except he owed Angelina more than anyone alive besides Tom Hickey, who adopted him.

Angelina had found him fallen on a sidewalk of Calle Siete. Two or three days and nights he'd lain in an alley wrapped in cardboard and quaking with a fever. When he realized, even while delirious, he needed to drink something or die, he pushed himself up, staggered a few steps, and fell. Then Angelina was kneeling beside him, on the floor of her windowless crib. She was pouring hot milk into his mouth. Little J.P. was rolling a toy car over him.

For almost a year, until the gang of street kids called Las Pulgas decided to kill him, Angelina had provided a mattress he shared with J.P. on the other side of a curtain from the half of the crib where she slept with her men.

A dozen years ago, when Alvaro returned to Tijuana and played guitar in dance clubs, where he and J.P. met Benny Luz, the only drinking joints in Tijuana's Zona Rio looked like the refreshment stands at little league fields. Their customers lived in the squatter shanties in the Tia Juana River flood plain. Then the riverbed became concrete, a wide and shallow canal. The squatters got chased to the city's outskirts. The Zona Rio developed museums, French cafes, business parks and Baby Love, a four-story octagon with a steel frame and amber-tinted glass walls. Given its patrons, Alvaro guessed the glass was bullet proof.

The bottom floor was a steak house. Up the glass elevator was the lounge where name acts from *el norte* entertained intimate crowds of the criminally rich. On floor three was the caged boxing ring. Above it was a place like the skybox at a ballpark, from where the maggots, without the annoyance of police or paparazzi, could bet on which boys would mutilate which other.

Alvaro stepped off the elevator onto Baby Love's third floor. The furniture was glass, chrome and black leather. A couple waitresses stopped chattering to stare at Alvaro as if questioning how many zillions of pesos he was worth. A bartender beckoned him over.

Her name was Elsa. She featured a square yard of bare chest and deep cleavage. Alvaro perched on a stool across the bar from her and asked for a double Sauza.

Rather than hustle after his tequila, she gazed into his eyes.

He said, "Juan Pedro."

She backed a step away and hardened her gaze.

"J.P. Ornelas," he said. "You know him."

"What if I do?"

"Get him here."

She turned and scampered the length of the bar then into a hallway down which he followed her far enough to see that beyond the restrooms was another door. She opened it, disappeared and shut the door behind her.

The cocktail girls looked to be rushing themselves and the only customers, two older men Alvaro had heard speaking German, and a redhead wearing sequins, toward the elevator. It arrived and whisked them off before Elsa returned.

When she came, two fighters escorted her. The bigger one had the pointed face and jagged teeth of a barracuda. He stepped to within six inches of Alvaro. In whispery Spanish, he said, "You want J.P. for what?"

"His mother sent me."

"Who are you?"

He reached up and patted the big fellow on the shoulder. "Alvaro. I'll come back in an hour."

A few hundred yards and a world away from the tourist zone on Avenida Revolución, on the corner of Calle Ocho and Avenida Niños Heroes, in a block of budget boutiques, Alvaro sat on the curb between the cart of a *helado* vendor and a kiosk of magazines and *fotonovelas*.

He remembered. He was eight. In a year or two, he might've run with Las Pulgas, mostly homeless orphans like he'd been until Angelina found him. A few of them were the sons of squatters who had built lean-tos out of wood and tin scraps, refrigerator crates or whatever, in the river basin or in the canyons up the mesa. They stole from the *mercado* and delivery trucks, snatched purses and peddled rolls of aspirin they claimed was Benzedrine, which they called bennies, along Avenida Revolución and in the nightclubs, to sailors and other drunken *gringos*. Or they lured *gringos* into cabs that would deliver them to motels where hookers disrobed them and called in the pimps and robbers.

Alvaro had only been eight a few weeks when the *gringo* sailor changed his life. In his memory, the *gringo* was a head taller than the others who poured out of the cab behind him. He looked like a werewolf from a *fotonovela*, and he terrified Alvaro even before he threatened to pinch his neck, lift his head off, and drop it into the sewer. But Alvaro didn't tell the giant the name of the kid with a bulging scar on his chin and a red swatch in his hair, or reveal the corner where they could find him. He gave the giant a phony name and the wrong corner. But somebody saw, and told Rey, the redhead, who was the *jefe* of Las Pulgas, that Alvaro had snitched.

J.P., who roamed like a ghost through the neighborhood and at six years old knew it all, came running and told Alvaro Las Pulgas was going to catch him and kill him. They meant to find him in front of the Jai Lai *palacio*, where Angelina's pimp stationed her boys with orders to seek out and deliver the drunks with the finest clothes.

Just after dark, Alvaro picked the lock on the trunk of an old Chevy with plates from California Norte. He ducked into the trunk, shut the lid and crawled up close to a crack between the fender and the wheel well. After the car started and drove for a long time then stopped and the motor quit, he kicked at the lid and yelled.

A miracle of fate or God delivered him into the hands of Tom Hickey, the kindest, toughest, wisest man he knew, who had come to Tijuana to buy new huaraches and firecrackers for his son Clifford.

For warning Alvaro, J.P. got stabbed by a rusty knife, six times. Las Pulgas would've killed him except a band of British sailors staggered into the alley and objected.

Ten years later, the same year Alvaro went to Vietnam, a man, a lawyer, who had known Angelina since the beginning, but lately had gone over to another *puta*, secured a green card for her. She gave up the life for a job as a hotel maid in San Ysidro.

Every time Alvaro came to Tijuana during working hours and had a few minutes to kill, he dropped in on Jaime in the pawnshop he had owned and run forever. Jaime was so old and his cough was so deep, each visit Alvaro suspected might be the last.

But Jaime still hobbled around, and still drilled him with questions in his Bugs Bunny voice, mostly asking for tales about Alvaro's women. Usually, Alvaro made up stories, though he could've told plenty of true ones. The old man would rear back, grip his belly and cackle. Today, when Alvaro admitted he was engaged, Jaime pounded on the counter with the side of his withered fist but stopped when he noticed Alvaro didn't smile.

Alvaro picked out a Beretta .32 caliber and the seven-bullet clip. About the reason behind the purchase, Jaime showed no curiosity or concern. By the time Alvaro reached the sidewalk, the transaction would be gone from the old man's memory.

Not that anything Jaime knew would matter. If Alvaro killed J.P., the *policia* wouldn't bother about him. They would leave that job to Luz.

Alvaro wondered how long he could evade the Luz mob if he fled to Alaska, grew a beard and turned it gray with worry, and drank everything in sight until he gained fifty pounds.

He found J.P. waiting on the Baby Love third floor. He was flanked by the fighters. The big one strode to meet Alvaro, raising his arms and curling his fingers to mean hands up. Alvaro complied. He got patted.

He hadn't seen J.P. since before Vietnam. At first he thought J.P. was sick. He looked gaunt, with sunken cheeks, and pale for an Indio. But his eyes were clear, and his voice was strong.

He didn't smile or reach for Alvaro's hand. He

said, "Okay."

Alvaro nodded.

J.P, said, "I'm here."

Alvaro watched the man's eyes. "Long time."

"No shit, lawyer. What's up?"

That J.P. spoke English, though his English was lousy, Alvaro interpreted as a message. J.P. was telling him they were living in a whole different world, as different people, than when they shared a mattress and worked the streets as partners. Long ago, they had signed with rival teams.

More comfortable with embellishing than lying straight out, Alvaro said, "Angelina's sicker than she lets on."

"Sick? What's this sick? She got cancer?"

"Maybe. In the brain. Some tumor. She's gone nuts. Sits in the dark and mumbles."

"Mumbles what?"

"Words I can't make sense of."

J.P. cocked his head, appeared to watch Elsa who flounced across the room to greet a trio of Japanese men in dark suits. The fighters held their gazes on Alvaro. When J.P. turned back, he said, "*Hombre*, I got my own problems."

It wasn't the words but the man's zeroed eyes that convinced Alvaro. A quiver at the base of his skull felt like a warning buzzer, telling him Don't slip. Show him the slightest hint you're the enemy, his gun will flash out, he'll deliver you to hell or wherever, then go wash his hands and get on with his day.

The thought of killing J.P. felt more ironic than wicked. J.P. was dead already. He already lived in hell. "Question?"

"Yeah."

"Suppose Luz told you to kill me. Would you?"

J.P. made a pfff sound. The fighters both chuckled, one deep, one twittery, and both gave Alvaro the look a question that stupid deserved.

"Don't fuck with Luz," J.P. said.

Alvaro nodded, not to J.P. but to himself, as he finalized a plan. He said, "I need you to sign papers. So I can get her committed."

"Give me the papers."

Alvaro shook his head. "You'd better see her first, make up your own mind. I'm not her kid."

J.P. made a loud, growling sigh.

Left alone with Elsa, Alvaro brooded over the double Sauza she had brought him. He thought about other directions life could've taken. Suppose the big *gringo* hadn't threatened him, or the snitch hadn't run to Las Pulgas. He might've gone to work for Luz and stood beside J.P. at the massacre. He might've hacked up a five-year-old with a machete.

Or suppose Vietnam, the tension, terror and

gore, had tweaked him a degree beyond what it had. Suppose he'd come home a touch more damaged or addicted and done some hideous crime. He wondered if Pop would kill him.

But probably his life wouldn't have gone those directions. Like Pop had told them often enough, the past has its ways of catching up. The son of a woman murdered by politicos because she wouldn't quit protesting, and of a musician killed in prison, and the adopted son of a detective who set his own rules and a woman driven mad by wicked men, should've foreseen his life would end in some bizarre yet fitting manner. Given the places he'd come from, the weird twist would be if he married a good woman and found a decent life. That he would get wasted by someone he crossed or spend the last half of his life on the lam, a guy with any sense would've seen coming all along.

J.P. wouldn't ride in the Camaro. Probably he knew that, once they were on the road, a gun might appear in Alvaro's hand. He might've even imagined Alvaro could be quicker than he was.

Neither would Alvaro ride with J.P. Besides the weapon J.P. wore under his coat, he might carry an arsenal in the trunk. Or kilos of whatever.

J.P. drove a Jaguar XJS. Alvaro followed. Along the canal, past the new arts complex and the *mercado* where tourists too rushed or spooked to venture any farther south bought their switchblades, Chinese stars, and other trinkets. Under the bridge and past the *frontera* proletariat lanes, which were stacked a quarter mile deep, J.P. pulled into the VIP lane. So he had crossing privileges. And a fine-tuned knowledge of the gatekeeper's schedule that assured he wouldn't encounter a customs agent who might decline to let him through without a search. The VIP lane only put them behind a limo, a rigged-out camper van, and a Lincoln.

J.P. vouched for Alvaro. He passed through the gate with a salute from the customs officer.

Alvaro pulled to the curb of Pepper Drive, across from the library. He parked behind the Jaguar. Climbing out of his Camaro, he recognized the last chance to change his mind.

He leaned both hands behind his back on the hood of the Camaro. As J.P. stepped out of his Jag, he peered in every direction. Then he walked around back of his car and stood tall in front of Alvaro. He motioned his head in the direction of the court.

Alvaro swallowed. If he tried to speak, he would choke. He shook his head. Then he stared in something like shame at the look J.P. gave him, which implied Alvaro hadn't the guts to join him.

As J.P. climbed the few steps, walked the path, turned and knocked on Angelina's door, Alvaro made as if his hands had stuck to the warm metal. The cottage door must've been locked. When Juan Pedro called out his name, Alvaro let go of the car, folded his hands on top of his head and squeezed.

The door opened. Three shots cracked. A woman began crying out to God, then another, and another. Soon neighbors came swarming. A siren chirped then wailed.

Alvaro thought of Elena and of the hardest moments he would ever endure. This evening, or tomorrow, when he would confess and watch her run away.

He pushed himself off the car and went to make certain Angelina had laid down the gun. Then he would meet the police, to assure them his client was harmless.

iv. OTIS

Way back, during an Arab oil embargo, Laurent Sozzani and I set off to cross the country in a 1946 Dodge pickup. On the way, we took notes. Later, I created Otis Otterbach, who turned those notes into a story, then a novella, then a novel, then a bigger novel, then an enormous novel (around 200,000 words). At last I convinced Otis to let Clifford Hickey and me edit it into a series of novellas.

"The Curse" and "The End" came to life during that long and arduous process.

THE CURSE

If you don't want to live, most anything could kill you — an acorn falling on your head, a summer cold, or eating the wrong kind of dinner.

My grandma said that, and chuckled, when I was fifteen. She could chuckle but I was scared and lonely already, knowing she planned to die soon.

Grandma was deaf and blind. She would hear if we shouted and her hearing aid was on. She could see blurs and some colors; pink to crimson was all rose and every light color was gray or brown.

Very early mornings, in time to catch direct sunlight through the east window of her studio, Grandma stumbled from her bedroom next to mine, made her way downstairs hanging on to the bannister, then tripped on the doormat as she walked outside. She wandered through the yard trying to hear jays and sparrows, smelling the eucalyptus, pines and mulberry trees she had planted fifty years before.

I shook myself awake, dressed and, to avoid my mother who'd be irritable from her migraine headaches and sleeping pills, I went through Grandma's room to the balcony, climbed down the rock chimney then walked up the hillside to the studio. Grandma was at her easel. She felt my vibration on the floor and turned around.

"Otis," she said, "is it green I've put on these mountains?"

"Yellow," I said. "You always put yellow where green ought to be."

Grandma smiled. "Then I'll simply make it springtime. It will be wild mustard on the hills. They can be hills instead of mountains."

I sat on the floor and warmed my feet in the quilt she kept there for me. Mornings had been like this since my father moved to Alaska and my mother and I came to live at the old house. Over six years Grandma had told me hundreds of stories about heroes, princes, fairy queens and prodigal sons, Trojan warriors, volcanoes, guillotines. Now she dabbed paint and told me about Joaquin Murieta, a murderous bandit from long ago.

Grandma said Joaquin had a fiery temper like mine was these days. A week before, I had demolished a chair after my mom said I had no right talking back to my Spanish teacher, because I was still a boy.

In old California, Grandma said, the Mexicans were driven from their land so Joaquin became wild with fury. He went out to rob and massacre. But a bounty hunter named Harry Love caught Joaquin, chopped off his head and carried it to Stockton where some merchant displayed it in a glass case and the citizens paid to look.

Grandma said, "One night in Stockton, Joaquin's sweetheart, Carmela, came to see him. She broke in late one night. She lifted the glass away and touched the hair, crying 'Joaquin, you have murdered me too. I must kill this Harry Love. Once I was innocent. God loved me, Joaquin.' Then she fell to her knees and covered her eyes, trembling because the head had begun to speak.

"Softly he said, 'God once loved me too, Carmela. And now Joaquin will not kill anymore. He will no longer fear the slaughter he does or hope it is a nightmare. Joaquin will not think about damnation. He is already damned. It is finished. Put his head in a box, Carmela, and throw it into the sea.'"

Once Grandma had been a dark beauty like Carmela. Even now her hair was black and her eyes sparkled, but her body was lumps and folds and her face was disguised in that wrinkled mask old people have to wear.

She smiled and asked me to tell her Carmela's story, because she knew I wanted to make up stories. But whenever I tried, as soon as I told the action to roll, the characters would stand still and glower at me.

Carmela could've killed Harry Love, but then

who would kill Carmela? Harry Love could've killed Carmela, then her brothers or somebody would've gone after Harry Love, but that seemed no closer to an ending.

Friday night, my girlfriend Nancy met me at the movies. Usually, as soon as the lights dimmed, I was on her with both hands, but this Friday I was thinking.

Grandma was disappointed that I couldn't make up stories, and I thought disappointment must be one reason she had grown tired of living. If I could make up a wonderful story about Harry Love and Carmela, she might take heart and want to live longer so she could teach and encourage me to be an artist like her.

I'd been tormented from trying to understand Carmela and Harry Love so I could decide what they should do. Now, I toyed with Nancy's thick black hair and watched her knee bounce until I discovered an idea, a feeling that sex might be at the heart of Carmela's story.

And I turned so horny it seemed a kind of madness.

I said, "Let's go get my car."

"You can't drive," she whispered.

"Watch me," I said, and told her I had a special permit you could get if you lived with an invalid who might need emergency transportation. I hustled Nancy out of the theater and up the hill to my house. She didn't argue or ask to see the permit. Even her guileless pose, I thought, must be a front for a brain full of wildness and larceny.

My car, an ancient Plymouth that had been Grandma's, was parked far from the house. My mother kept a spare key in the glove box. A few times I had used the key and gone for a cruise around the block.

The battery was dead. We pushed the car then rolled it down the hill. If I drove to the beach, I thought, with romantic waves and moonlight, I could convince Nancy to strip and go swimming. Then I'd be in business.

But as we passed the theater, my best friend Willy and Nancy's best friend Joan flagged us down.

They climbed in back. Joan fell on top of Willy and her skirt rode up. Willy had his hands on her thighs. The beach was twenty miles. I decided to get somewhere quickly. I drove to a hill just a few blocks away with a vacant lot overlooking the old granite quarry where Grandma and I used to pick mushrooms and give sandwiches to Mexicans camping on their way north.

When I parked near the cliff, Joan was panting and Willy had his hand up her skirt.

Nancy let me kiss down her neck, so I followed a bone ridge to her chest, loosed her top button with my teeth and tried to tongue down her cleavage, but she pulled my hair. "We're not alone, Otis," she whispered.

I wrestled her legs out from under her, but she kept her knees flexed as weapons, buttoned her blouse and leaned back against the door. I tried to pry her knees apart but she pinched my fingers with them.

"I'm just trying to get comfortable," I said.

"No, you're not. You're trying to get between my legs."

"If I don't, I'll fall off the seat."

"All right," she said, and let me between her knees. "But watch out what you try. I can tell you're excited."

"Bet he's got a hard-on," Joan said and giggled.

"Big deal," I said. "Tell her to shut up, Willy."

Nancy let me French kiss for a while then I worked my hand beneath her slacks. Her butt was quivering. "The seat's poking me," she said. "And my foot's bent sideways."

Joan giggled.

"Make her shut up, Willy."

"Screw yourself, Otis," Joan said.

I sat up and gave her the finger. Willy had her panties around her knees and his hand under the front of her dress. "She's got her panties around her knees," I whispered to Nancy.

"I do not," Joan said. "That's a lie."

"God, Otis," Nancy said. "You're mean."

I didn't feel mean. If I could've made her feel like I did, like somebody wrapped in cellophane, hot and panicked, if we could have the same heart and mind for just one moment, she would've stripped, been beautiful and sacrificed most anything to give us inspiration or comfort. And if we made a baby, she'd want to come live with me where Grandma could tell the baby stories.

But I couldn't even say I was sorry without choking on the words.

I climbed out and kicked the fender hard. Then I walked to the cliff and threw rocks over. They clanged on the wreck of a car in the quarry. When I snuck a look back, Nancy was combing her hair. It was no use trying to change anybody's mind. Thinking that was what made me turn mean.

I walked over and kicked Nancy's door. "Get out," I said. Then I kicked the back door and said it again. Willy and Joan crawled out, griping. I went around front and loosed the brake and gearshift then pushed the car a few feet until it rolled by itself. When the front wheels crossed into the air, the frame caught in dirt. It teetered for a while before it slid and the front end went straight down and hit the cliff. The rear end flipped. My car banged off the cliff three times before it landed in the quarry. I wanted it to blow up and burn, but it didn't.

"Damn. Jesus," Willy said. "That was a good car."

"You okay, Otis?" Nancy asked. She was holding me from behind and shivering.

"I'm sorry I laughed, Otis," Joan said.

"Lucky it didn't bounce that way," Willy said, pointing south. "It might've landed on a wetback."

I didn't say anything. While I walked Nancy home, she held my hand now and then, probably figuring I was a dangerous lunatic. I didn't bother to kiss her goodnight, and she ran inside.

On my way home, I thought about how funny Grandma used to look driving that car, because it was so much bigger than her. I remembered when a kitten hid in the motor and got chopped all to bits by the fan. At home, I climbed to the balcony beside Grandma's bedroom and listened to her gruff and ragged breathing. I thought, of all the billion people in the world she was the only one who would forgive me everything, no matter what.

Grandma wouldn't live much longer. That morning she had told me about a river valley where piles of dead leaves were magical castles, where there were pools of warm, clear water, tidelands everywhere and streams of sunlight that girls could walk up and pick fruits from the sky.

I snatched a sleeping pill from my mother's jar and slept late in the morning.

My mother was on the front porch. She shouted for me to come out. When I did, she slapped me. "The police called," she said. "They found Grandma's car in the quarry. You'd better have a good story, Otis, or I'll tell them to take you to juvenile hall, I swear."

"It was my car," I said.

"Did you drive at the cliff and jump at the last second?"

"Yeah," I muttered, knowing she'd yell just the same no matter what I answered.

"I know you were acting out a fantasy. Pretending to be James Dean?"

"Yeah sure."

She sat on the porch rail and shook her head as though she knew everything. "Otis, you know I don't like to talk against your Grandma, but this needs to be said. Those stories of hers are so dangerous, the way they fill your head with illusions. Look at your uncles." She meant Charley who built a sailboat that sank on its way to Tahiti, and Fenton who was getting his sixth divorce. "Or me, to marry a dreamer who goes off chasing oil wells. Otis, Grandma's stories are for children. Then you put them aside, or else they become a curse."

She stared at me and I stared back, for a long time, feeling as though I should defend Grandma or my father. But I didn't know enough. My ideas were like theirs, visions of how things should be rather than how they were.

"Did you tell Grandma?"

"Of course. It was her damned car."

I made a savage face and nodded until the nodding became a spastic compulsion, while I thought about Grandma with her eyes watering, her chest going heavy and pulling her down.

"Go on to Grandma," my mother said. "I can't do a goddam thing with you anymore."

I walked to the studio and sat on the steps, believing Grandma would probably clear my troubles by taking them on herself, and die even sooner than she would've otherwise, if she hadn't died already rather than see me again. I pounded my legs with a stick, then threw the stick at a bird and walked inside.

Grandma was there at her easel. "I've given up colors," she said. "They don't matter anyway. It's textures I'm trying for now. I know what you did. Otis, it was just something you did. We already know what you are." She pressed my chin between her fingers and smiled, meaning whatever I was, was all right to be.

"I'll tell you a story," she said.

"Once there was an older brother who had magical powers and a very young sister. They lived in the north woods. When the brother was about to die, he told the sister, 'Cut off my head and hang it over the door, then I can watch out for you.'

"Soon he died and the sister obeyed him. This was near a mountain where a great bear lived. He slept in his cave all winter, but when warriors came to hunt him he would wake up and kill them. Until one day a strange warrior appeared at the sister's hogan to ask for help with hunting the bear."

"Was the warrior named Harry Love?" I asked.

"All right," she said. "He was Harry Love. What was he doing in the north woods?"

"Running. Because he figured Carmela and a gang of Mexicans were out to kill him for whacking off Joaquin's head."

Grandma nodded in pleasure. "As they started up the mountain, an avalanche came. They found shelter under a ledge. Harry Love said, 'The avalanche has awakened the bear. Take my knife and cut your hand. Let the blood keep flowing and hold it high so the bear can't miss smelling it, while I stay hidden. Walk out lightly into the drift from the avalanche. Because you are small you will stay above the snow, but when the bear comes to take you his weight will drive him down, then I will come and beat him to death with my tomahawk.'"

Grandma's voice became raw and grim while she told how the sister helped kill the great bear. Then she skipped through time until, back at the hogan, Harry Love sat looking proud and giving orders.

"He told the sister to take her brother's head from above the door and burn it, but she refused. So he chopped off her head with his tomahawk. Then he set fire to the hogan and burnt both the heads. The sister and brother saw it all, from the smoke they had become together, because they had the same souls in their heads." With her eyes drifting, Grandma said, "I wonder what became of Harry Love."

She smiled dreamily and looked at me for an answer, but I only shuddered and asked, "Grandma, why do you tell me stories about whopped off heads?"

"Oh," she said, and thought for a while, "a chopped off head could belong to somebody who gets carried away, like in anger or when we are in love. And it could belong to a madman, an artist, or an old person who doesn't want her body anymore." She sighed and looked toward the window. "But I don't know why I tell the stories. If I knew, I would tell you why instead of telling the story."

That week Grandma got laryngitis. She couldn't talk and only painted an hour or so in the mornings. My mother wanted to take her to the hospital but she refused and said she was improving.

One night she started to choke. I got scared and even after she stopped choking I couldn't relax to sleep. I needed someone to share these troubles, a devoted ally, like a sister might be. My mother had no imagination, so she couldn't help me save Grandma. Besides, I wanted somebody to hold me.

Willy was the closest to a brother I had, and his sister Denise came closest to being my sister. She was only thirteen but mature for her age and a tease. She would brush my arm with her breasts and sit on my lap squirming until she felt what she wanted. Then she'd kiss my cheek and give a coy smile.

Thinking about her, I became wild and horny. Also, I thought she might help me with a story or give me some inspiration and comfort or at least she would take my mind off things, especially if we loosened up with wine.

I stole a few dollars from my mother's purse then snuck out and ran down the hill to the quarry. Three Mexicans were sleeping in the shack where the quarry office used to be. I woke one, which spooked him. Then he couldn't figure out why I was giving him money and saying "*Vino.*" I had to lead him across the road and point to the liquor store.

Once I had the wine, I followed a trail up the cliff

and over the hill, stopping to drink and trying to feel brave.

Denise's lights were out but her window was open. I jimmied the screen then reached in and shook her. She yelped. I told her to hush and said, "I can't drink all this Ripple myself."

She climbed out wearing baby doll pajamas, quivering with excitement, her hair still damp from a bath or shower. I followed her across the lawn to a sand pile behind the guesthouse. She sat and grinned and drank wine, with her shoulders pressed back so her nipples poked out.

"I never got drunk before," she said. "I'm glad the first time is with you, Otis."

She kissed my cheek and flashed her coy smile. Then I lay with my head on her lap, watching stars and thinking that if I knocked her up, Denise would make a perfect mother, young and happy with plenty of vigor. In places like Mexico, girls her age were always having babies.

I smelled something foul and asked, "What stinks?"

"Willy's superculture."

The superculture was a fishbowl into which, for a year, Willy had been tossing food scraps and boogers, armpit hairs and cigarette butts, worms and snails and flies, sweat, dingleberries, and toe jam. He thought it might create a new kind of mold or work to repel mosquitoes.

"My mom made him put it in the guesthouse. Boy, this Ripple tastes like Kool-Aid. Will it get me drunk?"

"That would take two bottles," I said.

She swallowed the rest and tossed it away, so I opened the other and handed it over, wondering how I could explain to her that it was a crime some people were older and some were younger and some people were sisters, and all those accidents of birth were supposed to keep us from doing what we could if we were the same age or strangers. But, I would argue, why should they?

"Otis? Maybe I drank too fast. Oh!"

I jumped up and led her to the Eugenia bushes. In the next yard was a catfight, then a big dog came woofing and the cats jumped the fence. After Denise threw up, she turned around smiling and humming a tune she'd forget and stop then start all over again. Then she crashed onto the ground.

The guesthouse door was unlocked so I carried her inside. The room was small and dusty with a double bed. I pulled back the covers and stretched Denise out beneath them. The superculture was fouling the air. I carried it out to the lawn.

I swallowed the last of the Ripple then sat beside Denise. I kissed her forehead. Her hair smelled like peppermint. I took a deep breath, lifted her arms and pulled off her pajama tops. She wasn't as plump as she seemed in clothes. Her breasts jiggled as she lay on her back with her legs spread slightly. I peeled off her bottoms and bent down to look. Not having seen a live pussy up close since I was small, I studied it a moment, contemplating its magic and danger. Then I got nervous and pulled the covers over her. I slipped under the covers beside her. I kissed her neck then lay still holding my enormous pecker. For all I knew it might split her in half.

I squeezed up against her so we touched all along to my knees where her feet reached. In her sleep, Denise lay her arm across me and gurgled then snuggled her hair against my face and said, "'Night."

I stayed there, warm and tingling, and thought about the hope just a touch from some people could give, until Willy opened the door.

He looked fierce as Harry Love.

I jumped up, yelping, "I didn't do anything. Swear to God."

"Maniac." He hissed and looked ready to attack me. "She's my sister, Otis, you pig. She's twelve and I ought to get my dad."

I wanted to scream that she was thirteen, that he had Joan to squeeze, and I deserved somebody. But all that would sound like begging. So I got mean and pushed him against the wall, then walked out to the lawn and kicked his superculture with my heel. The fishbowl broke. Stuff inside made a stream running toward the Eugenias.

Walking home, I tried to imagine anything that might help me feel less rotten and disgraced, but nothing would. Grandma couldn't help anymore. Even if she got her voice back and quit telling me about whopped off heads, her stories would be about kings and spirits and heroes, noble ones so different from what I had grown to be.

I stole a sleeping pill then slept until very late when the sparrows and jays had already quit singing and Grandma was dead. When I came into her studio she was slumped against the wall in the quilt she kept for me. The quilt was over her face. I sat beside her, stared out the window and made up a story. In my story Grandma thought, "The poor boy dressed in a man's body will find me cold and bloodless. I won't let him suffer that." So she walked toward the door, but the table got in her way. It was still morning. The sun was climbing, turning the smog crimson. There were mushrooms in the canyon beyond the quarry, she knew, wishing to see one for the last time. There were kids in the street kicking balls around, one of her favorite sights. But all she saw was blurs. So she crawled back to the wall by her easel where a great white bird was waiting. She petted the bird and kissed him, then she hid in my quilt and died. The bird took her soul and flew it away, to the golden boxes where the spirit that made us keeps the most precious things.

THE END

When the sixties ended, the weather changed. Fierce heat began in spring and kept rising. Through August, Santa Ana winds thrashed off the desert, knocking over cars in the mountains. They blew the smog out to sea but left something darker. Old nightmares returned. That summer a close friend overdosed on heroin. A grenade in Vietnam wasted my cousin Ward's leg. And in the hottest winds of August, a gang butchered Sharon Tate and five of her friends. Then a couple named La Bianca lay mutilated in their kitchen, and when the Manson family got exposed, two of them were girls we knew.

Denise wanted out of California. She said the Midwest could be a simpler, safer place. But I played guitar in a rock and blues band. After three years of rehearsing in a basement we were finally booking jobs, and now a guy from Zap Records had seen us and asked for a tape. So I wouldn't leave. Where Denise used to talk about our future together, now she confessed to thoughts about moving on her own.

One morning in October, she said we ought to forget our troubles for a day in Disneyland. We took the grocery money and inched north along the freeways in our old Chevy van with bald tires and burnt-out brake lights, hoping the place wouldn't be crowded, since tourists should've fled California, away from the heat and murders, while locals stayed home pointing rifles at the door. Yet they all were there, hordes of them, wiggling, licking ice cream bars as they pressed through the chutes. Perhaps Manson's capture had released them from anxiety. Or maybe Disneyland looked safer than home. Here you could laugh at the witches and ghouls. But I didn't feel safe. People kept staring at us. Denise appeared cherubic while I was tall and hairy. And since I had taken a capsule of mescaline our drummer gave me, I probably looked crazed. Yet where there are giant ducks and fairies, you don't expect to get stared at.

I stood in lines playing mind games, trying to levitate and make people disappear out of the line ahead. When Denise let a family cut in front of us, I poked her and grumbled.

She whispered, "C'mon, Otis, they want to be with their friends and they came all the way from Denmark."

We rocketed through space, crashed little cars into each other, rode a putt-putt boat through Utopias where all the world's children prove identical except for their color and clothes. We spun in big teacups until our guts churned. Finally I talked Denise into retreating to Tom Sawyer's island. I wanted to hide from the heat and the crowds, underneath a boulder.

So there we were, peacefully in line when a troop of Boy Scouts all turned and stared at me.

They stood on a raft from Tom Sawyer's island. Except that a few were darker, they looked like young Nazis in khaki shorts and all. I had a twitch of foreboding. Then the idea of getting spooked by Boy Scouts made me giggle. I put my arm around Denise. She was sweating and her T-shirt clung to her breasts. I told myself those boys were admiring her nipples and snug red shorts, though all the eyes still looked aimed at me.

As they swarmed off the raft, marched up the ramp, and pushed into the crowd, not for a second did the Scouts quit staring. They encircled Denise and me, cutting us off from the line. By instinct I stepped back against the cable that held me from splashing into the Mississippi, and I tried to glare them down. But they seemed a legion. My vision kept shifting from one pair of eyes to another. Some looked rabid, some watery and blinking. Others flashed in the sun.

Denise grabbed my arm and gave the Scouts her darkest scowl. "Hey," she said petulantly, "you guys knocked us out of line."

From behind me one of them bellowed, "Murderer!"

I wheeled around but got stopped halfway by a finger aimed like a gun at my face. The kid had red hair, freckles, and squinty eyes. He snarled, "You're Charles Manson."

A boy with no teeth yelled, "Who let him out?"

"He's on bail, stupid," a Dumbo-eared kid shouted.

One in the rear said judges were crooks and a boy with his cap on sideways hollered, "I betcha them bald girls broke him out."

I looked at Denise. She was staring like everybody else, including by now the whole crowd behind the Boy Scouts. Dads in beanies. Arabs with purple eyes. I saw cheeks pinked with rouge, faces from all over the world, sharp like beaks, Huckleberry Finn, a Chinese woman with a burr haircut, heads bowed in shame.

I tried telling myself this wasn't real, since nothing was, except energy. Still my heart raced and white noise filled my brain. I tried to hear music, peaceful melodies like "Ode to Joy." All that came was drum rolls and a Wagner crescendo. I panted through my nose, fixed my eyes straight ahead, and began to walk. The scouts and everybody parted as I staggered through a corridor of leers and silly, warped faces.

I heard Denise behind me declaring, "You guys are crazy. He's a foot taller than Manson. And ten years younger. His name's Otis and he's a peaceful man."

Dark shapes rose in front of me as I heard Denise yell, "Manson will never get out of jail, and I bet you kids spoiled Otis's whole day."

Ahead loomed two cops, one mustachioed, with a bell-shaped hat, fat blue suit, and shiny buttons. The other was a thick, hard, western sheriff. If they searched me, I was doomed, but I couldn't run when all around me stood a lynch mob. So I stopped, cold and trembling, leaned to my right and slightly forward, and with hands on my hips I gazed without blinking into the face of each lawman.

Finally they turned and walked toward a giant chipmunk beside the popcorn wagon.

Denise probably thought I'd wait while she finished bawling out the crowd, but I kept walking, gazing at my sandals and with hardly a thought except to get someplace alone in this treacherous world. I glanced up just enough to guide myself through another crowd and skirt along the edge of the lines before the Haunted House, where I was going to find some darkness. I ducked under a cable. As I moved to the front of the line, I only needed to show people my face and they stepped aside.

It felt like I'd done some unthinkable crime, too vicious to remember, and been expelled from humankind. I passed through the entrance. Nobody asked for my ticket. I turned left and marched into a room full of ghost laughter and portraits on the walls. One of them changed from a cat to a Southern belle and then to a withered hag. I saw no exit, except to go back. I whirled around just as the door slammed shut. The ghosts cackled. The floor began to quiver then dropped out from under me. My heart imploded. In a vision, I plunged all the way into Hell yet landed softly on my feet, near a door, which I slugged open with my shoulder and staggered through. To my left were little cars on a track, but I ran, staying close to the wall, dodging the busts of old patriarchs, past a door beneath an exit sign and through a ballroom where banshees wailed and green ectoplasm swirled, to another passway and another door. I fumbled for the handle, found and yanked it, heaved with my shoulder, and burst into a hallway full of amber light. Halfway down the hall, I sat on the floor, covered my eyes with my arms, and waited for the end. But lots of time passed and the end didn't come. Then I swore to go straighter and be kinder to people. Especially Denise. If a record deal happened, I'd treat her to a real honeymoon.

I sat there far longer than I knew. It took a long

time just to feel sure I wasn't Charles Manson.

Outside, the sky was grayer and the heat less foul, easier to breathe. It seemed fright had boiled the mescaline away. Still I walked carefully, my head lowered, eyes rising only to peer through breaks in the crowd. I found Denise between Frontierland and the Amazon forest, sitting on the root of a giant carob tree.

Her mouth sloped down, her chin crinkled and began to quiver. Then her arms folded tight across her breasts.

"I was so scared, Otis. For all I knew you might've got lynched but I didn't want to get a cop, with you holding weed. What could I do?"

I confessed how profoundly those Scouts had deranged me. Then we walked to Main Street where a trolley was just pulling out. We jumped it and squeezed onto the bench beside two nuns. Finally Denise looked up, kissed my cheek and took my hand, and pressed it against her bare thigh. As we clattered on, I spread my other hand across my eyes, because all along the sidewalk outside the shops and arcades, tourists wearing beaks or large ears pointed cameras at me.

I told Denise we should go to some office and demand our money back, but she said, "You'll just make a scene, and we'll lose. You can't beat Disney. Let's just get out of this zoo. Hey, and go to the beach for sunset."

Driving from Disneyland straight to the beach, you can get stalled by fifty stoplights, detours, and a traffic jam some collision has brewed, then you have to search between condos and mini-malls for the ocean. So we cut south on the interstate, bound for the cliffs at Dana Point, a place my cousin Ward and I used to surf.

The Sunday traffic was moderate, slowed to about thirty mph with gaps a few feet long between cars. We edged in and joined the show. Convertibles lurched by, jammed full of erect surfboards and girls, who wore mostly sunglasses, perched on the laps of pretty boys. Delivery men leaned forward over their steering wheels, arms up, shoulders hunched, like riders of the Pony Express. A few lunatics weaved in and out then horns blasted and people cursed each other and shot their fingers around. Denise said, "I think California's at least as weird as Disneyland."

For distraction and to lift my spirits, I asked Denise to play our tape, a copy of the demo we'd pieced together for Zap Records. The tape player was cheap, but that didn't excuse our music. The cut I sang, a fast, Elmore James blues, sounded so heartless I was glad when the tape player's batteries failed and my voice wheezed away.

Then we got stuck between a Highway Patrol cruiser and a '65 Impala lowrider, candy apple red with a twelve-foot antenna that flew the Jolly Roger. The skull wore a headband. Salsa music hooted over the freeway rumble. Heat waves steamed off the car tops. The sun reddened as it sank deeper into the hazy smog that capped the Laguna Hills. Then brakes squealed far ahead, and a couple dozen more brakes screeched, each of them closer. When the lowrider's lights flashed, I stomped the pedal and froze an inch from his bumper.

Denise and I sat gulping breaths.

A siren tooted then wailed, and came the red and blue lights to our rear. I cussed, kicked the firewall, and dug into my shirt pocket for two big joints. Denise wouldn't help, since she gagged easily. As I crammed them both into my mouth, I got lockjaw. To stall for time, I backed up far enough to edge around the lowrider then made for an exit, straddling the right shoulder at an idle.

"Swallow. Swallow," Denise pleaded.

But that weed absorbed my saliva and lay there dry as gravel. Still I managed to chomp, and finally to gulp. It squeezed like a tennis ball through a straw, so my throat felt like it was hemorrhaging. The cop, who had pulled over behind us, strode our way.

"Be nice, please," Denise said. She knew I'd lost

my patience, since every month or so I'd get rousted, usually on some pretext such as my van looked just like one stolen a few miles away. Then they'd search for drugs. The last cop made me remove the paneling, a half-hour job.

As I heard the cop's footsteps, I tried to look nice but eating marijuana made my face pucker. I turned to see him and reeled back. He looked like my cousin Ward, with ruddy skin and grayish eyes.

First he asked for my license and draft card, also Denise's license, and the registration. He questioned our origins and destination. He asked what kind of work I did and raised his eyes toward the hills when I claimed to be a musician.

The cop turned to Denise, leered a while, and commanded, "Open the back." He shot a glare and a smile of challenge at me, trying to goad me into saying something he could knock me on the head for. But I didn't make a sound, not even to protest while he searched the van, slinging our junk all over. Denise stayed with him to help. I scuffed barefoot through the ice plant telling myself this was no visitation, that God hadn't sent this certain cop to imply what a drugged, traitorous scoundrel I must be. Lots of men have big noses, ruddy skin, and eyes grayish-blue like the cop and Ward, I argued. But something tweaked inside me, and the darkest feeling rose. I'd only known such rabid shame once before, the week my cousin left for Vietnam. He told me about Vietcong tortures such as the many uses of rats and pits lined with sharp, poisoned sticks. Then his eyes drilled mine, like he'd spotted the enemy.

A few months later, in the only letter he sent me from Vietnam, he wrote, "I'm scared shitless. You're playing music. So how was Thanksgiving?"

Denise told the cop she had to pee or burst. She must've awakened his heart. With a brake light warning and one last sneer, he sent us on our way.

Across the boulevard, beside a 7-11 store, I pulled to an Exxon station self-serve pump. While Denise ran to the ladies room then back to the office for a key, an attendant came and stood close by. His face kept changing colors. I looked away, hurried with the gas and made for the men's room, just wanting to sit in the dark again. Until I slammed the door behind me, flipped on the light, and saw who gaped out from the mirror at me.

It sure wasn't Otis. With cavernous eyes, sharp bones and a pinched, hungry mouth, it looked like Charles Manson.

I dashed outside then bolted. My head throbbed and I couldn't see except for moving blurs, yet I survived the parking lot and reached the 7-11 store. But I couldn't make out things on the shelves, except large boxes such as diapers. As I wheeled around helplessly, a rescuer came, a small person fringed by a bush of auburn hair. Orphan Annie, I thought, and pinched my eyes. Next Peter Pan could fly in. But she asked what I needed, and as soon as I told her, swiftly she found scissors and Gillette blue blades with a free razor. She rang it up, two dollars even, and aimed me toward the door.

In the parking lot, two cars backed straight at me. I dodged and stumbled to the Exxon. By now my vision could focus enough so I spotted Denise inside the van, straightening things. I snuck past her to the men's room. I threw the sack into the sink and grabbed out the scissors.

The mirror rippled. The face behind it mocked me. My left hand trembled while I pulled the hair back into a ponytail. The scissors in my right hand, as I eased them toward the mark, swerved and nearly punctured my ear yet I got them in place, opened their jaws and chopped. A pound of the stuff fell on my back then wafted down to the floor.

I turned to the beard. Pulling it into little tufts, I began whacking and snipping. Before long only stubble remained. I was scooping hair out of the sink when Denise walked in.

She gasped. She stood with hands on her hips and her eyes misting, while I ran the water hot and lathered my face with mechanics' soap. Deftly, I guided a razor over hills and valleys and reamed the stuff out of sharp niches. I didn't even draw much blood.

When the razor slipped from my hand, I looked squarely at the creature who gazed down at me.

For three years I'd worn a beard, a mustache for six years. Before that, I was a boy. Now I'd gone pale. My cheeks sucked in. The upper lip hung down too long as if to hide big teeth. This fellow looked common, shy like he needed my approval, and sickly as though he might not live very long.

A feeble groan issued out of me. Denise came alongside and took my arm. She led me to the john, sat me down. She propped the door open with the waste basket and bent to work picking up hair while I kept still, exhausted, with arms on knees and face in hands, the sweat from my palms burning all that raw skin.

From there on, Denise drove. The sun had deserted us, leaving dusky, warm air that smelled of seaweed and gasoline. I lay in back touching my cropped hair and naked face. My head felt ready to spring off and bounce out of sight down the road. I used both hands to hold it on, while trucks battered us with their tail drafts and the van lurched when Denise hit the brakes, and lights kept sneaking in the window then flashing at me. Each of my senses seemed to split and fly off a different way until only my dimmest self remained, waiting for the end.

Finally I quit waiting and climbed up front. Denise hummed a Nutcracker tune. We crested a rise then looked down on the coast, straight at the mushroom domes of the San Onofre nuclear plant. They glowed orange, backed by the dead-green sea. To the south, from near to far down the beach, Camp Pendleton Marines bivouacked, their tents in clusters and landing crafts sunk in the tide. Then a great heap of sand exploded. Tanks bounded over the dunes.

But that didn't stop the surfers who angled in from north of the domes, rising out of the foamy peaks at the line where colors darkened as cool water from the deep met the atomic lagoon. The surfers looked to be on clouds, sky-riding toward the wild glory of heaven.

California, I believed, was either Babylon or the Promised Land.

"Too bad the radio's broken," Denise said.

I crawled to the rear and lay on the bunk. In dark, behind curtains and sunglasses, things got quieter. Cars breezed by. Our van's rear end quit rumbling. My breath didn't rasp anymore. For a while I felt lifted and dropped as by waves into their troughs, battered and tossed like plankton. Then it got quiet again. Denise carried me home.

Our place was a converted garage beside an alley in our hometown. It was only one room plus the bath, the patio, and garden.

I phoned my aunt to ask about Ward, expecting her to answer curtly, but she sounded friendly this time, as though she could tell from my voice that I now looked civilized. She said my cousin was learning to walk on his prosthesis, that he'd be home by Christmas, and she'd give him my love.

Denise volunteered to fix dinner. I took my Hummingbird guitar outside, sat on the table and played. I picked some high note runs that came out stiff and slow, as usual. So I turned to a new song, rhythm and blues. My part attempted to sound like horns, an ascending harmony line using three-note chords. Six or eight times I tried it, but the tangle of my fingers only got worse. To redeem myself, I chose "Shake a Hand," which Little Richard had done, the tune I sang best with our band because the notes fit my voice and the lyrics moved me. Yet I noticed the voice go hollow and flatten. It just couldn't rise with the feeling that lifted me. I stopped in the middle of the last verse. I stared at my reflection in the pick guard. The stranger raised his eyebrows at me.

When Denise came out with our tacos of Swiss chard and sour cream, I packed the guitar away then sat wondering if I'd lost my gift for music. And as the truth came, a taco slipped out of my hand and fell beside my foot.

Denise asked what was wrong.

"I just realized what a lousy musician I am."

"No, Otis," she crooned.

"I bet that Zap guy was drunk. When he hears me on the tape, he'll gag."

She touched my chin, lifted it higher. "Maybe it just sounded not so good on account of all that grass you ate. Honest, you're pretty good. Good enough. Remember when the Beach Boys first started, you surfer guys used to pelt them with eggs and stuff. Look what happened to them."

"I don't want to get pelted. I want to do something good," I groaned. "I want to find out what I can do. Maybe even who I am."

Then I couldn't talk anymore. I got an urge to go lie in the dark forever. To fight catatonia, I stood up and walked to the alley, then cut east toward town. Straight ahead, about halfway up from the horizon, a few stars blinked reddish then burnt back to silvery, yet remained brighter than the others. I wondered if they could be pointing our way to the Midwest or beyond.

Denise appeared beside me. I stared at her face, with the deep eyes and parted mouth that, not always, but sometimes, spoke just the right words.

"You're Otis." She pressed me to her side and whispered, "Otis is more than a good man. He's a great story, too."

V. ETC

ABOUT THE STORIES

Cars

My dad was a truck driver. He loved fast cars. When I was fifteen, he died of a heart attack. Too soon afterward, my mother got stricken by spinal meningitis. The doctors consigned her to months in an isolation ward. During her absence, my best friend, Eric, a remarkable fellow I suspect to this day may have been an angel, moved in and stayed with me. Soon after my mom came home and Eric moved out, he flew out of a car and died.

My first draft of "Cars" had Bingo dying in his crash. Then I decided to keep him alive but lost as a confidant and mentor, and the story came alive for me. It felt more true to life after I left the facts behind.

Ophelia in Death

After I'd finished my first novel and found an agent, my wife Laura and I flew to Europe. We hitchhiked here and there until we landed in Athens, where I took a job as a substitute teacher at an American school.

We lived in a small town on the Bay of Marathon, and made friends of some Navy folks stationed at a communications station. One of them was Bob Middleton, a charming and crafty fellow.

Laura left me and moved in with Bob. Susan and I rode the school bus together. She was in tenth grade, a pure delight and pristine beauty, rather like Faust's Gretchen. Way too young and innocent for a tainted fellow like me.

"Ophelia in Death" is a sort of ode to Susan.

The Murder Game

A dear friend contracted Hepatitis C. He lived in Ocean Beach, where I used to hang out long ago with my cousins Virgie, Wendy, and Wade. Their dad owned a grocery on Newport Avenue.

Wade, the oldest, was both brilliant and rebellious. He drove a hotrod Ford yet (according to my grandma) scored highest in the nation on a college board exam, which earned him a full scholarship to MIT. Later, he would buy a sailboat, take an extended vacation, and never return.

His sister Virgie was a splendid beauty, outside and in, with a queen's poise and grace. At Point Loma High School, she was chosen as most attractive and nicest, all three years. Her tragic flaw was a fascination with outlaws.

Here's a poem I wrote about her.

WARNER SPRINGS

Outside in the mineral pool, our mothers
one widowed, one divorced,
they and the kids float and splash.

Our cousin Stevie, orphaned last year,
he and I slouch against the wall between
the swinging doors and the jukebox while
Virgie, two years older, ages wiser,
like the girls on American Bandstand
or in news clips screaming their vows
to Elvis--Virgie reigns here in the rec room,
commanding obedience with her poise, silky
hair,
tight pedal pushers, bare feet, fleecy
sweater, short sleeved and pink.

A boy with glossy hair, his chinos
pleated and pressed, has won her favor.
Stevie and I twitch and squirm. They dance
belly to belly, to "Twilight Time."
Because we too are boys, we know of his plot
to steal her away in his shiny car. If we could
we'd banish him from the world but
we're only thirteen.

The jukebox lifts the record from the turntable.
The boy's hand is low on Virgie's back as
he steers her toward the far door and his

chopped
Mercury painted to match
Virgie's scarlet lipstick and nails.

But she knows everything. She spins
toward us, dismissing him
with her royal smile. He freezes.
Only his throat moves.
He's swallowing a lesson
about class, as in classy,
about family.

The Light

This one's mostly true. So close I included most
of it in *Reading Brother Lawrence*, a memoir.

Then and On Earth

Jim Thompson's life was largely shaped by the
Great Depression, as were so many of my parents'
generation. So when Judith Moore, my editor at the
San Diego Reader, asked if I could give her a story
about Jim Thompson in San Diego during WWII, I
said, "Wow. Cool."

The Enemy

Sylvia Curtis, mother of Eric whose strength and
goodness I have tried to capture in *Reading Brother
Lawrence*, told me wonderful stories about

218

downtown San Diego during WW II.

"The Enemy" began with one of them.

Too Sweet

Margaret Beasley was my friend from second grade on. Her singing always amazed me, as did her way of being top in the class in most everything except sports yet showing not the slightest vanity.

Right out of high school, Margaret's gifts got discovered. She moved to Hollywood and sang on television. I spent a week visiting her. That visit inspired "Too Sweet".

Mama's Boy

On a trip to Mexico, Henry Mikkonen, Ron Maxted and I befriended a shoeshine boy. He wanted to live in the U.S. So we tried to bring him home with us. The border patrol objected.

Later, Steve and Bev Havens adopted the son of a housekeeper who had left him behind when she returned to Mexico. He was a remarkable athlete and a great friend to Sam Havens, until some troubles sent him home to Guadalajara, where he died.

Alvaro Hickey gives me the opportunity to honor those two good fellows.

The Curse

When I was two years old, my dad's cabinet shop failed. We sold our home and moved in with my grandparents. My mother, an 8th grade English teacher and my dad, now a wholesale meat salesman, worked long hours. So my grandma cared for me, which was a profound blessing.

She was a poet and a landscape painter of the California Plein Air school. My favorite occupation was lounging with a cat on the sofa of her studio, listening to the stories she loved to tell and watching while she daubed layer upon layer of oil paints onto a canvas until chaparral and desert came to life.

The End

It was I who got accused in Disneyland, by a Boy Scout, of being Charles Manson, and I who found refuge in the nearby Haunted House, where I recall thinking, "Okay, I'm not Charles Manson, but who in the world am I?"

A Request from the Publisher

If you appreciate Ken Kuhlken's stories, please consider composing a brief review and posting to the online site of your choice.

ALSO FROM HICKEY'S BOOKS

by SUSAN SALGUERO:
The Gachi. She wasn't the only angry woman at U.C. Berkeley. Always on edge but unaware why, she knew she had to flee. A passion for music delivered her to Spain. There she staked her life on Flamenco.

by JARED BROWN:
Million Dollar Man. A phone call from a neighbor reporting a suspicious character at his home sends Jared Brown, a family man and Christian psychologist, to the outskirts of hell.

by ALAN RUSSELL & KEN KUHLKEN:
No Cats, No Chocolate. Mystery authors launch an adventure with high hopes and dreams of winning the fame they're convinced they deserve, as guests on a national television show. An Amazon #1 bestseller in several categories.

by OLGA SAVITSKY:
Shockabonda. Writers often imagine their ideal reader and compose accordingly. The reader Olga Savitsky chose was God. Since she wasn't likely to fool her

reader, she needed to be real.

by KEN KUHLKEN:

Midheaven. High school senior Jodi McGee turns from drugs and boys to Christ, but soon thereafter falls for her English teacher. As a result, tragedies test her will, her faith, and her sanity. Finalist for PEN's Ernest Hemingway Award for best first novel.

Reading Brother Lawrence. During a troubled time, novelist Ken Kuhlken discovered a certain book helped him find peace. *Reading Brother Lawrence* chronicles his search for understanding.

Write Smart. Much acclaimed author Ken Kuhlken shares insights gained over thirty-some years as a novelist, university creative writing professor, and founder of Perelandra College. By following the Write Smart process, writers will efficiently create, revise, and sell their stories.

Writing and the Spirit. Anastasia Campos declares: "With all the ease of a friend on your couch — an ingenius, multiple-PhD-holding, wise-man sort of friend — Kuhlken combines observations of the world we live in, writers in history and his own experience (failures and triumphs) to form an all-around handbook of writerly wisdom."

by NICOLE L RIVERA:

Finding Unauthorized Faith in Harry Potter. Nicole L Rivera, Creative Team Manager for the fansite MuggleNet, marries faith with fandom in this wise and compelling devotional. Drawing on the Harry Potter story and parallels from the Bible, she reflects upon life's deepest truths, about faith, friendship, courage, loyalty, and love, and provides us with the keys to living like Christ and the Harry Potter heroes.

Hickey's Books provides support for the **Perelandra College writing programs** in the effort to enrich popular literature and writers' lives. Learn more at: perelandra.edu

BE A CALIFORNIA EXPERT

The **Tom Hickey crime novels** are riveting stories that also offer a vivid and panoramic vision of California as it transforms from a frontier to the most influential place on earth.

"Elegant, eloquent, and elegiac, Kuhlken's novels sing an old melody, at the same time haunting and beautiful." Don Winslow, author of *The Cartel*

Readers who accompany Tom and his extraordinary family on their adventures enrich their knowledge of history and the dark and bright recesses of the human heart.

"Tom Hickey is one of detective fiction's most original and intriguing creations." *San Francisco Chronicle*

The Biggest Liar in Los Angeles: (L.A. 1926) Unless a famous evangelist will take skeptical Tom Hickey into her confidence, he may never learn who lynched his friend.

A San Diego Book Awards Best Mystery.

The Good Know Nothing: (L.A., Tucson, and McCloud, CA. 1936) A famous novelist, an outlaw who may be the Sundance Kid, and publishing magnate William Randolph Hearst stand between Tom and the truth about the disappearance of his father.

Los Angeles Book Festival Best Mystery Award.

The Venus Deal: (San Diego, Mount Shasta, Denver, Tijuana, 1942) A gifted jazz singer leaves her job at a San Diego nightclub, in which Tom is a partner, to avenge the crimes of a spiritualist guru.

.

The Loud Adios: (San Diego, Tijuana, 1943) While Tom serves as an M.P. on the San Diego/Tijuana border, he discovers occultist Nazis plotting to make Baja California a German colony.

St. Martins Press, PWA Best First P.I. Novel

The Angel Gang: (Lake Tahoe, San Diego, L.A., 1950) An L.A. mob's beef against Tom results in the kidnap of pregnant Wendy Hickey. Tom alone can't rescue her, but if he can enlist the help of angels ...

The Do-Re-Mi: (Rural Northern California, 1971) The Hickey's adopted son Alvaro, a musician booked at a folk festival, flees from a murder accusation. His brother Clifford's best chance of proving him innocent requires the help of the victim's girlfriend, one of the hippies known as Jesus people.

Shamus Best Novel finalist.

The Vagabond Virgins: (San Diego, Rural Baja California, 1979) A heavenly apparition appears in Baja California.

While she rallies the faithful to overthrow the corrupt Mexican government, Alvaro Hickey gets the call to join her crusade.

Visit kenkuhlken.net for special offers.

ABOUT THE AUTHOR

Ken Kuhlken's stories have appeared in *Esquire* and dozens of other magazines and anthologies, been honorably mentioned in *Best American Short Stories*, and earned a National Endowment for the Arts Fellowship. He has been a frequent contributor and a columnist for the *San Diego Reader*.

His novels are *Midheaven*, a finalist for the Ernest Hemingway Award for best first novel, and the Tom Hickey California crime novels — see page 202 above.

With Alan Russell, in *Road Kill* and *No Cats, No Chocolate,* he has chronicled the madness of book tours.

In *Writing and the Spirit* he offers a wealth of advice to writers and everyone looking for inspiration.

Reading Brother Lawrence follows him on a trip to the Kingdom of Heaven.

He resides on the web at kenkuhlken.net and hopes you will visit and use social media and newsletter links and keep in touch.

In the physical world, he lives near the Pacific Ocean and the U.S.- Mexican border with his Zoë, to whom he dedicates this book.